KU-595-777

SCOTTISH
SHORT STORIES

Scottish Short Stories, now in its fourteenth year and volume, acts as a sensitive barometer of the times as well as a forum for all that is new and exciting in Scottish writing today. As Deirdre Chapman remarks in her introduction, the emptiness, both geographical and mental, which was a prevailing theme of recent years has given way to a gritty, wry examination of lives and lifestyles, of individual choices and dilemmas. Chance and accident loom large with fortune or unfortunate consequences, and the world seen through the writers' own and their creations' eyes, appears as something of a puzzle.

It is a rich selection we have here: a tapestry of places – Mexico, the South of France, the Hebrides, Egypt – and a range of different voices to match, from the Glasgow dosser about to be reunited with her son to the last deliberations of a fastidious detective. As usual there are new and gifted writers among the established favourites, and the result is a collection which will surprise, intrigue and impress in the best traditions of this series published jointly by the Scottish Arts Council and William Collins.

SCOTTISH SHORT STORIES

1986

Introduction by Deirdre Chapman

COLLINS
8 Grafton Street, London W1
1986

William Collins Sons & Co Ltd
London · Glasgow · Sydney · Auckland
Toronto · Johannesburg

First published 1986

Family Holiday © William Andrew 1986; *Pearl* © George Mackay
Brown 1986; *Swan Song* © Moira Burgess 1986; *Maturity* © Kirk-
patrick Dobie 1986; *Krakatoa, East of Java* © Maureen Duff 1984;
Mossy © Audrey Evans 1986; *The Board of Governors of the House of
Charity* © Patrick Farnon 1984; *Incident in Le Lavandou* © Ronald
Frame 1986; *Henry and Joyce and the 33-year-old Woman* © Alex.
Hamilton 1986; *The Beautiful People of Juan Les Pins* © Iain Mac-
Donald 1986; *Dool* © Lorn Macintyre 1986; *Summer Fish* © Catriona
Malan 1986; *Scarab* © Ian Rankin 1986; *Our Lady of the Pickpockets*
© Dilys Rose 1986; *The Travelling Poet* © Iain Chrichton Smith
1986; *Confession at Altitude* © Alexander McCall Smith 1986; *The
Snark was a Boojum* © Ian Spring 1986; *Henry's Bottom Drawer* ©
Valerie Thornton 1986.

The Publisher acknowledges the financial assistance of the
Scottish Arts Council in the publication of this volume.

British Library Cataloguing in Publication Data

Scottish short stories 1986.
1. Short stories, English — Scottish
authors   2. English fiction —20th
century
823'.01'089411 [FS]   PR8675

ISBN 0 00223075-5
0 00223076-3 Pbk

Photoset in Monophoto Imprint by Ace Filmsetting Ltd, Frome, Somerset

Printed and bound in Great Britain by
Robert Hartnoll (1985) Ltd.,
Bodmin Cornwall

CONTENTS

INTRODUCTION

'Twenty years ago it was not difficult to earn a living as a short story writer. Now, it is virtually impossible': Neil Paterson in 1973 counting out the British and American periodicals which had failed and introducing the first volume of *Scottish Short Stories*. Its arrival just as the reading public had begun to wander away from short stories and while writers with the acceleration to bring them back were, in Scotland at least, largely concerned with poems, was a display of Scots disdain for the apparent climate comparable to Osgood Mackenzie's exercise with palm trees at Inverewe. Never mind the wind, feel the Gulf Stream.

Neil Paterson explained the series' philosophy in the first preface. 'We may never be able to do enough for the short story reader, but we are determined, over the years, to find ways and means of priming the pump for the short story writer.' Consider, then, the pump and what comes up. After fourteen years the reservoir of slack talent and bottom drawer stories is long gone, but shortage is not a problem. Two hundred and forty-eight stories were submitted for this collection. Does the pump create its own supply?

In 1986 the short story is part of the repertoire of a breed of Scottish writer who may be equally familiar as poet, novelist, critic, dramatist, occasional entertainer, writer in schools, libraries, centres of excellence, community centres – and perhaps, before long, shopping centres. He is any or all of these things in order to survive as a full-time writer. He has raised the standard of short story writing and brought a more discriminating audience. Inevitably, though, he risks spreading himself thin, and short stories are seldom accommodating to a writer whose current focus is elsewhere. Promised subtleties made explicit or left obscure under the pressure of a deadline can only leave the reader with a sense of regret.

Regretfully, then, Stewart Conn, Ariane Goodman and I agreed to exclude several writers we admired but whose stories showed signs of other work in the pipeline. It is a point to note, though, that if all the 'names' who submitted had sent their best work there would not have been room for them in this volume.

If the pump has stirred things up for the writer, from the consumer's point of view the supply looks healthy and assured. New sources are keeping up the pressure. Many memorable stories were sent by writers unknown to us, and several are included in this selection. Their work had a freshness of theme and approach and gave unexpected glimpses of the world through the eyes of a reflective minority.

If subject matter was job-related as often as it seemed, school teachers predominated, their themes variations on the dilemma of involvement. Of these 'Mossy' handled it with greatest economy.

Urban low-life, violence, despair, excess in all its forms and the effects of these on children accounted for the largest area of concern. The theme often seemed too strong for its writers and is therefore under-represented here. To lay aside writing so powerfully experienced because of a quibble about style often felt like passing by on the other side, though the difficulty was usually in the writer's own sense of impotence. If some of these writers can cultivate detachment or a clearer stance they have a lot to contribute.

It was interesting that what is essentially social workers' casebook material has edged out the traditional examination

of emptiness, geographical and mental, as the most popular subject, the problems of too much replacing those of too little. Those stories with a rural setting were more often concerned with the flaws of such a life than with its celebration.

The middle-class mid-life crisis was another favourite theme. Here the sexes seemed fascinated by each other's problems, women as well as men pacing out the executive power struggle, while men looked in mirrors through women's eyes. In 'Incident in Le Lavandou' Ronald Frame shows a capacity close to William Trevor's to identify with older women as they dissect and reassemble themselves. Reading stories of this category it became apparent that the sex of the writer betrayed itself in an odd way. Men, writing about the other sex or their own, were preoccupied with appearance. Women gave little thought to it.

Structurally, the standard of entry was high. The element of questioning, perhaps the single quality that most clearly marks out a potential writer, was detectable in a surprising number of stories. Many more failed from an inner pomposity. The consciously literate were the most tiresome to read along with those who experimented ponderously with language and those who took two sideways leaps for every step forward.

The stories we have selected succeed on several levels. 'Dool' yields its complexity at the careful pace of its characters. 'Krakatoa, East of Java' weaves threads of contrasting textures while holding to a final shape. 'The Board of Governors of the House of Charity' has a taste and a smell but lingers particularly like a dark oil painting uneasily remembered from childhood.

Our final selection is geographically perverse, going twice to the South of France, to Mexico and to Egypt while neglecting Scottish urban squalor with the single exception of 'Swan Song'. This is largely the result of three editors, who might each have chosen a representative selection,

pooling their preferences, and is, in fact, our guarantee of fairness. Since we were not compiling the *Scotsman* calendar but trying to do justice to the intention and the sustained performances of a variety of writers, our choice is as random as their themes.

Haggling was amicable and similar to judging a beauty contest. Beyond our shared first preferences (five) we found common ground where the first list choice of one or two was to be found on the second list of the other two or one. If this sounds obscure, in practice it is the simple mathematics of compromise that leads to Africa and Asia vanishing by the last seven of Miss World, leaving South America over-represented.

In practice, too, it left each of us mourning the literary equivalent of unexpected eyebrows or a memorable walk, while happy to welcome back an uneasily rejected early choice. Special pleading was also allowed on an equal basis. If it is of any consolation to writers not included, we would only have been satisfied with a much more cumbersome book.

The span of submission date to selection meeting coinciding with the Scottish summer break, I took my 248 stories on holiday. Foreign writers I met were much impressed that people of the calibre of George Mackay Brown and Iain Crichton Smith have no ego problems about sharing covers with unknowns, and that we have new writers able to appear in such company. This is a very democratic volume.

Wherever you read it I hope you will find in it the balance of spontaneity and structure that makes the good short story a complete experience.

FAMILY HOLIDAY

William Andrew

The old man was studying the crossword when he heard the steamer's approach. The deckchair his son had set up for him on the grass above the shore was beginning to make his scrawny buttocks ache, and the glare of sunlight on the page blurred the clues and squares and seemed to drain the words of meaning, so he was glad of the distraction offered by the throb of the engine and the beat of the paddles.

Shading his eyes, he searched the smooth water beyond the little bay, but saw only a few boats moored for fishing and a distant island shadowy in the haze. The sounds were closer now, and came from the left. 'A steamer, Ian!' he called to his son, who sat reading on a boulder near the water's edge, his balding head and too much of his stout body exposed to the sun. The old man pointed towards the low, wooded peninsula at the end of the bay, and his son stood precariously balanced on the boulder, his sunglasses pushed up on his head. A family picnicking nearby stopped talking and children playing on the sand looked too.

But the steamer did not appear. Instead the sounds began to recede, and soon the people on the shore lost interest. Ian jumped down and came to him. 'A steamer?' he asked.

'Yes, I heard the paddles. I can't hear them now. It must have turned.'

His son squatted beside the chair, on his jowled face the tolerant smile he kept for the more amusing of his parents' eccentricities. 'Dad, there hasn't been a paddle-steamer in these waters for sixty years or more.'

'It's what it sounded like,' the old man said, already wondering if he had made a mistake.

'More likely someone's outboard or the water-ski boat from the hotel.' The old man frowned, but was afraid to argue. To change the subject Ian took the newspaper and glanced at it. There was a smell of sweat and sweet sun-oil about him, and the top of his head had begun to blister and peel. 'Do you think four-across might be "detergent"?' he asked as he handed the paper back. 'Deter and gent.'

'I suppose it might be,' the old man admitted. Ian rose, patted his father's shoulder and strode back to his boulder and his book. Reluctantly the old man wrote the word in, dismayed yet again by how hard he found it to confine the letters to their squares.

'What's happened, Richard?' he heard his wife call from behind him. Nervous of the effect of the sun on her skin, she liked to sit alone in their son's car to read or knit or sleep. Now she was enjoying a pleasurable anticipation of disaster. 'Has there been an accident?'

'No. Nothing like that,' he called over his shoulder.

'What?'

He twisted round in his chair to reassure her but she was at the door of the car, immediately behind and above him, so he could not see her. 'Everything's all right,' he shouted as loudly as he could, and then coughed with the effort.

'What are you saying?' she asked impatiently.

He saw the picnickers hiding smiles, so he said nothing more, hoping his stillness could calm her. He heard the car door close. The combination of her deafness and the recent weakness of his voice was making public conversation a problem. It would be easier if she would sit at his side or if she did not resist his offers to keep her company in the car.

So here we are, he thought, the three of us strung out equidistantly between the road and the sea, separate, hardly communicating. With some envy he looked at the family seated at their picnic, sandwiches being passed round, conversation and silences comfortably mixed, and he remembered the tall, blonde girl who for eleven years had been his daughter-in-law, and who now lived far away with his two grandsons. She would not have allowed this loneliness to blight the last day of the holiday. She would have coaxed or bullied Ellen out of the car, and she would have had Ian building sandcastles with the boys. There would have been banter and laughter, and fruit and sweets, and a sense of a day worth storing away.

He stared at the slouched, sun-reddened figure of his son and wondered again why he had not been able to keep the affection of that bright, bossy girl, and what quarrel or incompatibility he had measured against the loss of his children. The old man sighed as he remembered how easily *he* had made every concession demanded of him to keep his family together.

And now that family was together again, father, mother and son, sharing a house as they had when Ian was a child, but with the optimism of those days replaced by ugly undercurrents of disappointment and resentment, as a middle-aged son thrust his private bitterness into the already difficult old age of his parents. For most of her life Ellen had ruled generations of schoolchildren and her own household with zest and efficiency. Now there was someone else helping to pay the bills, and he had to be considered and consulted before decisions were made, and that some-one was her son, whom she still thought of as a child or at best a foolishly rebellious adolescent. Ian, on the other hand, had known years of independence and his own home, and could not be expected to take kindly to being a son again, regularly reminded of how childish failings had grown to adult faults and criticized for his clothes and his drinking. There were frequent rows, harsh with recrimination, in which the father tried to mediate or insert a humorous quip to defuse the situation. But usually he failed, and the fight went on with renewed vigour, leaving him depressed by his own inadequacy.

So perhaps he should be grateful that for the moment mother and son were separated by their books and several yards of shore. Yet he knew he might have prevented much of the trouble if he had spoken out strongly when Ellen was encouraging Ian to ease his maintenance problems by coming to live with them, or earlier when she had taken her son's side as the first danger signs had showed in his marriage. Or earlier still, in his own marriage, when his affection and respect for her had induced him to sit back and let her take charge of all their lives. He sighed again, shifted himself into a more comfortable position in the chair and let his eyes close. Just before he fell asleep he heard again the distant pounding of the paddles, distinct in spite of the cries of the playing children, and smiled to think how wrong Ian had been about that.

Later, in their hotel room, Ellen said, 'A paddle-steamer! Really, Richard!' She was sitting at the dressing-table, pushing more hairpins into the already glinting bun on top of her head. At eighty, she was proud of having kept her hair, her plump figure and her wits about her. A year older, thin and stooped, he knew he was not doing nearly as well.

'I'm surprised he told you,' he said, though he knew that talking about him provided an area of truce which they both sometimes welcomed.

'He was concerned.' She looked hard at him in the mirror. 'He said other people on the shore heard you.'

'Yes, I think they did,' he admitted. Deciding that that had been said to hurt, he added, 'But you didn't. Are you going to wear your hearing-aid at dinner tonight?'

This earned him a reproving glance. 'Indeed, I am not,' she said calmly. The last hairpin went in, and she surveyed the effect left and right, and cupped the white wad of hair in her hand to assure herself of its neatness. 'I wouldn't need it at all if people spoke clearly.'

The dinner gong rang while she was making up her mind which brooch to wear. She did not hear it, but he waited for a couple of minutes before suggesting it might be time to go down. The determination with which she dismissed her disabilities was impressive, and showed that the sinew within her which he had always loved and needed was still there. It was a will to survive that he had seldom shown, except, he thought, in his choice of a wife.

There was little conversation during dinner. His taunt in the bedroom inhibited him from bellowing inconsequential remarks across the table, and Ian seemed lost in his own thoughts. At last Ellen said, 'How must we look? Three people with nothing to say to each other but, "Pass the salt, please," and "Another fine evening". What has happened to us as a family?'

Irritably Ian came out of his reverie. He leaned close and enunciated very clearly. 'I'd be glad to discuss any topic with you, Mother, if it didn't mean broadcasting to the entire dining-room.' Her lips tightened. 'What was the point of Dad and me getting you a hearing-aid, if you won't use it?'

'It doesn't work properly,' she snapped.

'It's meant to go in your ear,' he told her. 'It's not designed to work from your handbag.'

The arrival of the waitress to take away the plates delayed her answer to this. It was their usual girl, cheerful and red-haired, and Ian and she exchanged a smile which was held just too long. When she had gone, Ellen said, 'I gather you'd rather ogle the waitress than make civilized conversation with your parents.'

Loud enough for her and neighbouring diners to hear, he said, 'If I thought the conversation was going to be civilized, I'd give it all my attention.'

And that was that. Teacher and lawyer lapsed into stony-faced silence, while the retired salesman, whose livelihood had once depended on genial small-talk, was afraid to risk a public rebuff. He turned his attention instead to the view from the window, where, beyond the empty deckchairs on the lawn, the sun was beginning its descent into soft clouds banked on the horizon. It promised to be a spectacular sunset, and he hoped Ellen would remember their ritual for the last evening of a holiday.

And she did. After dinner she put on her coat and a headscarf and came with him for a stroll along the shore near the hotel. It was very still. The glassy sea, alive with the pink and mauve of the sunset, unfurled tiny, silent waves to darken the shingle at the water's edge, and the only sound the slow, crunching rhythm of their footsteps. This was how over the years they had ended each holiday, walking arm in arm, whatever the weather, to watch the last sunset. He was glad she had wanted to continue the tradition, but sad that she had brought her grievances with her.

'He was terribly rude. I'm sure everyone heard him.'

'It doesn't matter. Let it rest.'

'Oh, Richard, that's always been your way. The line of least resistance.'

'He's going through a bad time. The divorce. Not getting that partnership. We must be patient.'

'But why take it out on me?'

'Look, Ellen, some of the guests are out in the hotel boat. It'll be a good night for fishing.'

For a moment they watched the outline of the boat, black against the vivid water. A match was struck and sputtered as a pipe was lit, and then all was still again.

'He was making eyes at that waitress, you know.'

'Are the midges bothering you? Shall we walk on?'

'And every night after we go to bed, he's down in the bar. What will that do to his professional reputation?'

He led her towards the jetty. 'He has to make his own way, Ellen. If, missing Val and the boys the way he does, he needs a night's drinking and chatting with the locals, that's his business. I doubt if any of them knows what work he does in town.'

'That's not the point . . .'

'Look at the colours, Ellen,' he interrupted, not liking the way their voices were damaging the silence. They sat close together on the edge of the jetty as the light exploded slowly up the sky past the fading layers of cloud to touch the wisps above them. Rose petals thrown high and frozen. 'There was a time,' she said softly, 'when you would have painted that.'

He shook his head. 'No, never sunsets. They're too elusive.'

'You were good. Why did you stop?'

'A Sunday painter, whose brush no longer obeys him.'

She leaned closer and tightened her grip on his arm. 'We are very old, Richard,' she whispered at last. 'Much older than either your parents or mine lived to be, and your sister and most of our friends are gone. Are you afraid?'

'Sometimes,' he admitted. She had turned to watch his lips in the half-light. She nodded and laid her head on his shoulder. He wanted to add, but she might think it too sentimental, that he was not afraid of anything at moments like this.

'We must go on fighting it,' she said. 'That's why I nag you about drifting into the past. If one lets memories take over one's thinking, the awareness of *now* goes. And you must nag me too. We must help each other.'

He put his arm around her, and as they sat there, he heard the steamer again, the thud of the paddles, the surge of water at the bow, loud, loud, in the silence of the sunset, and they were waiting on a pier with Ian small between them and the queue of returning holiday-makers around them. Their luggage was at his feet and Ellen, healthily tanned, her fair hair tousled and faded by the sun, held their return tickets ready in her hand.

Ian had heard the steamer before anyone, and cried, 'It's

a paddler, Daddy! Which one do you think it is?' Already the black smoke of the funnel showed above the headland. 'Go on, Daddy! Guess!'

'The *Jupiter*?'

'No, I bet it's the *Waverley*! What about you, Mummy?'

Practical but laughing with them, Ellen said, 'I don't care which it is as long as there's room for us and it gets us home safely.'

'Richard?' she said, peering at him, and the sounds of the steamer disappeared. 'Were you off in the past again?' she accused gently. He smiled and shook his head. She smiled too, touched his hand and said, 'It's getting cold now. We should go back.'

As they approached the hotel, an imposing baronial building, whose windows still gleamed with the sunset's dying colours, Richard tried not to remember that somewhere behind those windows was their son and the future. With infinite sadness he felt Ellen grow tense at his side, and by the time they entered the foyer, she had withdrawn her arm from his. Ian saw them from the bar and came to meet them, his manner conciliatory when he said, 'Come on, you two, let me buy you a drink for our last night here.'

Ellen was coldly over-polite. 'Not for me, thank you. I have the packing to do. But you stay, Richard, if you like.' It was one of those awkward moments of choice they occasionally gave him, and when he indicated that maybe he ought to accept the invitation, she shrugged and climbed the stair, stiff-backed and a stranger again.

In the tartan-and-oak bar they took their whiskies to a corner table where Ian could keep an eye on all that was going on, the darts match, the noisy arrival of a group of forestry workers and a young man reverently removing a piano accordion from its case. 'It's going to be a good night, Dad. You should stay and see what happens.'

'No, thanks. I'll finish this and call it a day.'

'Scared of Mum?' Richard frowned and Ian's grin

18

faded. 'Forget I said that, and I'm sorry about what happened at dinner, but that deafness game annoys me.'

'She's resisting old age. You should admire her for it.'

'Not when she's doing it at the expense of my nerves.' For the moment he seemed to forget about the rest of the room. 'Oh, Dad, I should never have come home. Even if all I could have afforded was a crappy bed-sit somewhere, I should have kept my independence.'

'Your mother wouldn't have liked her lawyer son living like that.'

'That's just it!' The old man saw the trapped desperation in his son's eyes, and felt a surge of love for him. 'When Val left, Mum begged me to come home, and as soon as I did, she started to make my life a bloody misery, picking at me, goading me, as if I were some kind of threat. What's it all about, Dad?'

'I've never understood,' his father said miserably, 'but it takes two to make a fight.'

'I know, and I hate myself for rowing with her, but I'm forty-three, and I can't be her little boy again, meekly adapting to her moods and expectations of me.'

'No, I know you can't.'

'And I can't be you.' They both felt the reproach of this hang between them. Ian smiled sheepishly. 'Not that it can be much fun being you once Mum and me get going.'

'Listening to the two people I care most for in all the world tearing at each other. No, not much fun,' Richard thought, and then wondered if, after most of a generous whisky, he had said the words aloud.

He was reassured, however, by his son's expression which had shifted all too easily to self-pity. 'It's not much fun being me either,' he announced mournfully. 'On a career plateau. Half my income going to support a family I can see only by arrangement. Constantly provoked by an old lady who seems stimulated by fights that leave me exhausted and guilt-ridden.'

Richard was going to tell him that he was still a young man and would move on to a more interesting phase in his career and probably remarry and learn to see his mother in perspective again, to say everything he had meant for months to say, but Ian was no longer listening. He had seen someone come into the bar and was trying to disguise a furtive signal of greeting. Richard turned and saw the friendly, red-haired waitress, now transformed into a night person by a tight, green dress and a mask of pale make-up. Quickly he finished his drink.

'No, Dad,' Ian begged, contrite, 'you mustn't go yet. Let me get you another whisky.'

'One is my limit,' Richard protested mildly, 'and I really ought to go up and help your mother. Enjoy yourself,' he added, embarrassed to see boyish guilt on a middle-aged man's face.

Ellen, of course, did not need his help. She was methodically folding and packing the soiled clothes as carefully as the clean, and he could tell by the briskness with which she moved that there was no way he could revive the relaxed companionship they had shared on the jetty. In fact, there was something new and agitated about the way she was working which alarmed him. Holidays had always been her special pleasure, planning them, saving for them, booking them. Even the chore of packing usually gave her some enjoyment, but not this time. He sat on the bed, his head spinning from the effects of the whisky, afraid to speak in case he said the wrong thing.

'Was Ian drunk?' she asked at last, not looking at him.

'Of course not.'

'Was the tarty red-head there?'

'I didn't see her,' he lied uncomfortably.

'She will be. What is he thinking of? Where is his professional dignity?' She shook her head in despair.

By the time they got to bed there was a full-scale ceilidh in progress downstairs, songs and dance music and general boisterousness. Richard wondered if she could hear it. She was lying very still, unnaturally still, far on her own side of the bed, and he knew she was not asleep. Surely the din was too distant to disturb her or remind her of her son's social indiscretions. Surely after their walk along the shore she would soon fall asleep.

Suddenly she sat up and switched on the bed-light to look at her watch. 'It's after midnight, Richard,' she said angrily. 'Go and see if Ian is in bed yet.'

'No,' he replied with unusual firmness. He imagined himself finding Ian and the waitress in bed and explaining to them that Ian's mother wanted to be sure he was getting his rest.

'Then I'll go,' she said. She rose and, because her dressing-gown was packed, put her raincoat on over her night-dress.

'No, Ellen, you mustn't!' He got up and staggered round the bed to her.

'Someone has to keep tabs on him.'

'Ellen, come to bed and let the boy be.' He grasped her shoulders and was shocked to see how white and wild-eyed she was. This was not the woman who had snuggled against him and warned about the dangers of letting the mind wander.

She wrenched herself away from him. 'That's always been your way, hasn't it! Let the boy be. And look what he's become!'

'He's no longer your responsibility, Ellen. Please come to bed and forget about him.'

But she wasn't listening, and this time no hearing-aid would have made any difference. She was in an anguished world of her own. Hands clasped as if in prayer, she asked herself, 'What am I going to do? How can I make him a son to be proud of?'

These questions chilled him even more, because they were an echo of her reaction when, as a child, Ian had let her down in some way, had lied or failed an exam or been late for a meal. He had to make her see they were no longer appropriate. 'You must let go again as you did all those years ago.' But, of course, she never had and that was the problem. She stared at him, as if from a great distance, eyes strangely unfocused, and he knew she was ill. She backed to the door. Loudly and urgently he cried, 'We must help each other. That's what you said. So listen to me, Ellen.' But she turned on her heel and left the room.

He thought of going after her, but knew that a few paces would take her to Ian's door, and there was nothing he could say or do in a public corridor that would stop her. Instead he got back into bed, hoping the warmth of the covers would ease the shivering brought on by her unsettling behaviour. He prayed that Ian was already in bed, alone, or that he was still downstairs and would never know about his mother's brainstorm.

And it seemed that one of his prayers had been answered when she came back and said, 'He's not in his room.' But then she added in her best schoolroom voice, 'I think it's time someone suggested he should be, don't you?' Once more the door shut behind her.

'Ellen, no!' Now his imaginings were nightmarish. Ellen, her hair hanging loose, her coat held closed over her nightdress, her feet pushed bare into her travelling shoes, marching into the crowded bar to tell her son he had stayed up too late. This time his prayers were for miracles. That she would catch sight of herself in one of the mirrors on the stair and see how foolish she looked. That the receptionist was still on duty, would see that she was unwell and waylay her. Or that she would trip and fall, not too badly, and people would think she had mistaken her way to the bathroom.

But downstairs a song faltered and stopped. He moaned aloud as he pictured the shared humiliation taking place below, and then switched off the light so he would not have to see her face when she returned, for he knew how cruel Ian's tongue could be when he had been drinking.

A few minutes later she slipped back into the room, closing the door quietly behind her, and in the darkness he heard her drop her coat on the floor and kick her shoes off. 'Ellen?' he said. 'Ellen, are you all right?' She did not answer, but as she climbed into bed a sharply broken intake of breath told him she was weeping. He moved to comfort her, but she pushed him roughly away. Downstairs the resumed song ended to loud applause, and the accordion began to play a reel. Clearly above the music he could hear her stifled sobs, and he shed tears too, for her and for himself. It was long after the ceilidh had ended and Ellen's breathing had lengthened into gentle snoring before he fell into a fitful sleep.

In the morning neither of them referred to the incident, but it was there in the silences between them, and in the care she took dressing for the journey, so that they were late for breakfast, and in the knot of fear in his stomach as they went down and he anticipated mother and son meeting again. At Ian's place at table, however, there were crumbs of toast, the remains of a boiled egg and a used coffee cup, so there was a temporary reprieve, helped by the fact that the red-haired waitress was not on duty. As they ate, they talked safely about the drive home, how long it would take and the prospects of good weather offered by the heavy dew on the lawn and the haze on the sea.

Only once did Ellen refer to the night before. With lifted chin she ended a longish silence by saying, 'I was quite right to do what I did last night. Quite right to be concerned.' Realizing how important it was for her to believe this, he agreed, and noticed with pity the troubled look which replaced her defiance.

After breakfast she went to the reception desk to pay their share of the bill. There had been a time when she would have insisted on handing him the money so that he could pay, a reminder, almost certainly unintentional, of how little he had contributed towards it. Mercifully she now preferred the honesty of paying it herself, so he was free to go upstairs to carry out his only task of their departure, to make sure that nothing had been left in their room. Knowing that she would secretly check up after him, he took great care to search the drawers and wardrobe and all other likely hiding-places.

It was as he was reaching behind the mattress for a possible spectacle-case or book that he became aware of raised voices in the distance. With a jolt that made him hold on to the bed for a moment, he recognized the voices and knew that they came from Ian's room and that if he could hear, others could too. He hurried out and along the corridor past a maid too casually dusting nearby, as Ellen shouted, 'You did it to make me look small, didn't you?'

And Ian replied, 'What about what you did last night? It was grotesque!'

Quickly Richard let himself into the room. Mother and son faced each other a few feet apart like pugilists, the man flushed with anger, the woman pale. Richard was relieved to see that it was normal bad-temper that had control of his wife, not the lost rage of the previous night. Neither of them seemed to notice that he had joined them.

'To pay the whole bill by cheque,' Ellen cried, 'that was a deliberate insult.'

'So you keep saying. I don't see it. You give me your share in cash and that's us square.'

'Oh, no, it isn't! This way you play the big man who takes his poor old parents away for a holiday, and I won't have people think that's true.'

'It's your pride that's hurt, isn't it? You have to be in charge. You have to call the tune. Well, *my* pride was hurt last night, I can tell you!'

She folded her arms, headmistress-fashion. 'I want you

to go straight downstairs now, please, and ask for your cheque back, and for two separate bills.'

Ian laughed. 'Not on your life! I don't want them to think there are two loonies in the family.'

They glared at each other, eye to eye, like two cats on a wall oblivious to everything but their own confrontation. But they had reached a momentary impasse, and the old man, his heart beating wildly, knew that this was his chance to intervene, that he owed it to them and himself to do so as firmly as he could. He cleared his throat, and said, 'When will you both realize that life is too short to waste arguing about things that don't matter?'

It wasn't the strong statement he had wanted to make. It had come out trite and querulous. But he hoped it would be enough to break the course of their quarrel.

They both turned to him, and their almost identical display of the pain and anger and exhilaration of battle frightened him.

His wife said coldly, 'This is a money matter, Richard, so it hardly concerns you.'

His son's smile was contemptuous. 'Where were you last night when she decided to do her sleep-walking act? Thanks a lot, Dad!'

He felt his whole body contract with shock, and above the roaring in his head he heard Ellen shout, 'Don't speak to your father like that!'

And Ian yelled back, 'Why not? You do!'

Then he was out of the room and stumbling downstairs, and their voices seemed to follow him. He came out into the dazzling light of the morning where people were going about their lives normally, putting cases into the boots of cars or carrying deckchairs out to the lawn. He shuffled on-to the grass, which was slick and treacherous with dew, and found a bench at the farthest corner of the garden, facing towards the sea. Sinking onto it, he listened to hear if the terrible anger of those voices reached even there.

25

But there was only the fast beating of his heart and the softer rhythm of the waves. A violent shudder shook him, and a groan which he tried to suppress. Then there was another sound, matching the beating of his heart, the thud-thud of the paddles of the steamer in the quiet of the morning, distant as it had been the day before, but coming closer.

He leaned forward, peering eagerly out to sea. And there it was, pushing proudly along the line where the smooth water met the mist. He saw the rush of spray at its bow, the smoke streaming back from the tall, narrow funnel and twin wakes creaming the sea behind its raked stern.

Triumphantly he looked about him to share the sight with someone, and he found that at last he was not the only one who saw it. They were all there with him in the garden of the boarding-house on the Firth. Papa stood and shaded his eyes to watch it, Mama under her parasol looked up from her book and smiled indulgently at the excitement on her son's face, and his sister, kneeling on the grass in front of him, was distracted from the daisy-chain bracelet she was making.

Across the water they could hear a band playing merrily on the deck, and people lining the rail waved to them. He thought he could hear them calling out and laughing. 'Wave,' Papa said. Mama said, 'Wave to them, children,' and showed them how. They all waved and then laughed when a white plume of steam rose from the funnel and a second later they heard the steamer's siren give a brief hoot of greeting above the churning of the paddles.

Ian, hurrying across the lawn to apologize, stopped abruptly, and Ellen, watching from the bedroom window, put a hand to her mouth, as they both saw the old man wave at the empty sea and felt the chill of knowing that something had happened which could not be reversed.

PEARL

George Mackay Brown

A day in winter. No school. I was sent from the smithy to the boathouse with a message. It was this: *John Gorss the ferryman is not to trouble Tessa Smith again by night or by day, winter or summer, to his peril.*

I said this four or five times till I had it perfect. Mistress Smith was my tutor. Ollie Smith muttered, 'Too bad. . . . A pity, a pity. . . . No need for that. . . . Jack's a fine boy.'

And Tessa, in the next room, snivelled and wept.

'There's a penny,' said the old woman at last. 'There'll be another penny when you get back from that trash of a boy, and a piece of gingerbread. A boatman indeed! Tessa's made to be a farmer's wife.'

I walked through new soft-fallen snow. Purple grey clouds prowled in the north and east.

What would he say or do to a boy reciting that rigmarole, John Gorss the ferryman? He was as quiet and silent as a seal, a remote sea-loving young man.

John was not at home.

I said like a packman in the door to the kind old lady at the boathouse: *John Gorss the ferryman is not to trouble Tessa Smith again by night or by day, winter or summer, for his pearl.*

'Who sent you to say this?' said old Scilla Gorss. 'A pearl? What's this about a pearl? Tessa Smith – is that the blacksmith's lass? So that's where the bold boy has been going every night since Hallomas? I wondered, I can tell you. Did that fool of a John give her a ring, or something? That old harridan. Did she tell you to say that? A slut she is and always was, Topsy Smith. Sending a boy through the snow with a rigmarole like this. You better come in, boy. Let me see, you'll be the youngest boy at the Mill now. Am I right? Like your father as two limpet shells you are, boy. Come over to the fire. I'll give you a mug of warm ale. I'll have a thing or two to say to that Jack. So that's what he's been planning all winter, eh? I see it now. To take that little mouse of a thing from the smithy to rule at this hearth and board! I have to laugh. Me – what is supposed to become of me? Tell me that, boy. Sit over there on the rocking-chair, boy. Take the cat on your knee. Turnip-top like boys. The ale will be warm in one minute. Tessa, is that her name? I have to laugh. What does she know about this shore? Has she ever dried a fish in her life in the chimney smoke? Could she tar a boat for him? And that old slut of a mother – her whose grandmother sold laces and spoons at the doors – she has the brass impudence to send a message to the boathouse by the mouth of an innocent boy. Well, of course, the poor baggage can't read or write, I expect. Or the postman would have been with a letter. She has to send a small shivering boy through a blizzard. Oh, Lord, the things I could tutor your tongue to say to her, in reply to this piece of impudence! Look through the window, see if you can see John's boat out there. The *Rainbow*. No, well he needn't hurry, there'll be a worse storm inside this house when he *does* get back than ever he saw out there. I have a tongue in my head. The deception! A boy I rocked in his cradle and nursed through measles and croup and a broken leg – yes, and fed though I went hungry myself, after his father was drowned. Yes, and clothed. Timothy Gorss, that was my man's name, a better man by far than this John of mine, though I say it myself. Drowned he was, out there, in front of my very eyes, on a windy morning in June when the sea was blue and white and black. Well, be that as it may. A pearl? Did she say a ring or a bangle? Don't burn your tongue, boy, the ale's hot. Well, where was I? If it wasn't that I have such rheumatics in both legs, I'd set out this very afternoon to give that trollop a piece of my mind. Yes, I would, snow or no snow. I could say things would make her man's anvil silent a long while. Who or what or whatever does she think she is? For one thing, I would tell the slut that Tessa would not cross this threshold in marriage with John Gorss, if I could help it, no, not for a dowry of a thousand pounds. (Where am I to sleep, I wonder, after the wedding – in the attic, eh, above the rafters?) John Gorss will answer me that before this night is out. Boy, would you like a dry fish or two to take home with you? Your father always liked a smoked haddock. I wonder if nobody has ever told the ignorant baggage that she is that I, Priscilla Anne Gorss, was five years lady's maid over at the Hall, to old Mrs Susan Sweyn that's been gone (God rest her) forty years come Lammas. Mrs Susan Sweyn trusted me and treated me, boy, as if I was her own flesh and blood. I got her clothes to wear out, and her shoes too, for we had the same footlength. I ate with her many an afternoon from the same platter and board. And, "Priscilla," she would say, "you've learned gentle ways and manners here with me at the Hall," she'd say, "and you won't be wasting your life now on a simple ignorant boatman!"....' But I wasn't going to stand for that, boy. Dearly though I loved Mrs Sweyn, and combed out her hair like a harp every morning, I said, "I'm sorry, ma'am, but I love Timothy Gorss, even though he smells of the sea and can't read or write, and has rough ways with him...." Do you know this, she wasn't angry with me at all, for all the bold way I had spoken? No, boy, but when I married Tim after harvest she gave me a purse with five golden sovereigns in it. Yes, she did. And I was free to visit up at the Hall whenever I wanted. Yes, and the good kind woman came here once or twice, and the last time she was here she told me that, in her opinion, as far as she could see, Tim was a good honest man, and I had done well to marry him, though I had moved into poverty. And when peedie Jack was born, she sent down a silver cup for to celebrate the christening. There it is, boy, over there, on the dresser, between the two blue willow plates. (And I suppose that little mouse of a Tessa will think she's entitled to the silver cup, too. As if a pearl wasn't enough. She's got more thinks coming.) Must you be off, boy? Well, it seems to have stopped for the moment, the snow. You could get home between two showers. I'll wrap up two fish for your dad. Tell him I ask for him – I sat in the school with his mother, your granny, I did. I just wish you could be here to see John Gorss's face when I face him with his deception and his hidden ways and the things I've done for him every single day of his life. A pearl? I wonder if the poor fool of a boy saved up his few shillings to buy her a pearl ring in Hamnavoe? I wouldn't put it past him. . . . A pearl? They can keep it. A poor cheap imitation thing it'll be for sure. Well, boy, it's done me the world of good, your words and your company. You come again, any time. Would you put down the cat and take another look through the window? Oh, there is a boat in the Sound, is there? Well, well, well. My Jack – I'll give him pearl. Don't slip in the snow, will you? That's a good boy, step canny all the way. It'll come to a hard frost – I feel it in my bones. . . . Now, then, tell me this, will you be seeing that poor ill-put-on creature at the Smithy? Did they tell you to come back with an answer from me? Well, boy, I'll tell you what I want you to say. You'll say this – *I gave your message to Mistress Priscilla Gorss. She said nothing at all. Not one word. She listened and she smiled and she shut the door.* . . . Do you think you'll remember to say that? That's a clever boy. Say it just once more. Fine. Where's my purse? You deserve twopence for your cleverness. I would like to see the slut's face when you say that! Wheest. . . . The keel on the stones. But, Jack. . . . I have a plan. It just suddenly struck me. I'll say nothing to Jack either, when he comes in.

I will not open my mouth from the time he lifts the latch till the time I go to bed. Not a syllable or a breath. That'll make the creature wonder, if anything will. I usually have the day's news, such as it is, all ready for him, and he tells me what's been happening in Hamnavoe and thereabout. Not this night. Silence. His old mother dumb as a stone – that should bring him to his senses. Not that he ever had much wit at the best of times. Now, boy, don't lose your twopence. Put it in your pocket. All the way back to the smithy, repeat what you have to say to the old hussy. *Mistress Priscilla Gorss listened and she smiled and she shut the door.* . . . A pearl, indeed. They can keep their pearl, so long as that handless thing of a girl stays forever from this door.'

But John Gorss and Tessa Smith were married the following May, in the Manse, and there beside each other stood Mrs Topsy Smith and Mrs Priscilla Gorss, along with a score of other friends and relations. Mistress Smith dabbed her eyes every now and again during the ceremony, and that tear-drop was the only thing about the whole business that, in my judgement, remotely resembled a pearl.

SWAN SONG

Moira Burgess

Lizzie reached back into the stinking darkness of the archway and her thin dirty hand closed with glee round a splintery chunk of wood. Grinning, she rammed it into the red heart of the smoky little fire. 'You'll can tak' him tae the cleaners, Belle,' she said.

'She wouldny dae that,' cried Mrs Weston, all worried, 'an' him her only wean!'

Her fat shoulders heaved in emotion like the wave of the sea, and the trapped and mingled scents from her three greasy coats wafted eagerly into Belle's face. Belle turned away.

She disguised the turn, though, by making it into a rummage among the possessions in her cardboard box, all neatly stowed for the day. She disentangled her comb and a jagged triangle of mirror, and ostentatiously tidied her straight flyaway grey hair.

It was an act, because she'd been up at six, when Lizzie and Mrs Weston were lumpy bundles of rags spluttering in their sleep, and to right and left in the caverns of the other archways the rest of the dirty old buggers wheezed and groaned. She'd had to keep darting her eyes about as she took her clothes off, in case one of them was awake and ready to enjoy the show. Hell mend him if he was, nae time for the baths the day. She washed her small taut skinny body, bit by bit, every inch, stiff with goosepimples in the sharp little wind that probed up off the river in the dawn. She held her head grimly under the jet of rusty water from the standpipe. She kept her hair cropped short on purpose for quick drying. It stuck out now like a bloody bottlebrush, being so clean.

'Aye, ye'll need tae look yer best the day,' tittered Lizzie the bitch.

'I wonder have ye changed much, Belle, over the years,' mused Mrs Weston, who was just a pure fool.

'I wonder has he,' snapped Belle. She shut her mouth tight, since even that was more than she wanted to say to those two. Thirty-two years an' three months, she could say, and watch Mrs Weston's eyes brim over at the thought: I suppose he's learned tae wipe his ain backside by now.

Lizzie leaned on her elbows and gazed into the roof where the pigeons strutted their funky stuff, jerking their tails to squirt the girders white and green. 'D'ye mind Mag Divers?' she innocently remarked.

Belle compressed her lips and put her comb away. She shrugged into her raincoat, made for a six-foot man, and pulled the felt beret down over her hair.

'Every day ootside the Grand, hail rain or shine. Carried a soup-tin for the takin's so she did. Just the one lassie, been Stateside for years, same as your Johnny.' Lizzie waited for some answer, which she didn't get.

Mrs Weston raptly jumped in: 'Cam' back tae fetch Mag hame wi' her!'

'But Mag's no' there,' said Lizzie, glancing at her with a twisted grin. 'Naebody sees hide nor hair o' her for three weeks. Day her lassie sails for hame, there she's back ootside the Grand wi' her soup-tin.'

Mrs Weston was quite distressed. 'Maybe she took no' weel. Aw, would that no' be like the thing? Maybe she was groanin' in her bed an' her lassie searchin' high an' low – '

Lizzie looked this time, deliberately, at Belle. 'She wis daft,' she said. 'Sure she wis?'

'She had nae pride in herself,' said Belle, biting off the words.

That shut Lizzie up, but not for long. Nine struck

tinnily from the church, standing awkward and alone in the rubble of its glebe. Belle shivered: any minute now . . . Lizzie noticed, and said sweetly, 'Ye'll need tae watch, Belle, that he's no just after a housekeeper on the cheap.'

Belle took a deep breath. 'I ken whit I'm worth,' she said. 'My ain room an' a telly. Maybe an allowance. I'll gie him my terms.'

'It shouldny be like that,' Mrs Weston grieved, but her voice was lost under Lizzie's: 'That's right, Belle, I telt ye, tak' him for every cent he's got – '

Across the lovey-dovey moans and the gloating, Belle said curtly 'If it's him.' She paused; this time she really had shut them up. Quiet and wondering, speaking to herself, she said, 'An' if it's me.'

They both flew at her on that.

'Sure it's him. Sure it's you. Sure the welfare wumman checked it a' oot when she seen the ad.'

'There's hunners o' Isabella Smiths.'

'Aye, but yer address,' said Lizzie impatiently, and Mrs Weston piped up 'Yer maiden name – '

'He wouldny be sure o' the one,' said Belle, 'an' he wouldny ken the ither. How would he? He wisny two.'

'But there's papers, sure there is,' said Lizzie the know-all, 'when you foster a wean away.'

Belle drew a breath of hate. 'It wisny exactly official,' she said, 'whit I done.' Eleven at night, the knock on the door, bundling Johnny in his blankets, dumping him in the woman's shaking arms greedy for a wean. Bright blue eyes slitting open for a moment, but he was sound asleep, pink face under the sweaty-damp curly hair: 'Oh aye, he's likely changed a bit!' she screamed at Lizzie, who looked, no wonder, quite amazed. To cover herself she ducked her head and scrabbled inside the jerseys under her coat. 'There's this bloody stupit photy thing,' she said. 'The welfare wumman dreamed it up. He's tae bring his an' I've tae bring mine.'

34

'Aw, a photy!' That was right up Mrs Weston's alley.
'You an' him when he wis a wee shaver. Aw, the nice. I've
got one an' a'.'

'Allow you,' observed Lizzie, but she grabbed it all the
same, inquisitively inspecting the back; though she was
out of luck as usual, nobody got to know Mrs Weston's first
name. The photographs went from hand to hand, but finally
Belle had them both. Black and white, of course, being
thirty years old: two lassies in back greens, smiling babies
in their arms. Mrs Weston overweight even then, and her
hair, fair or maybe reddish, a mass of curls. Still was, when
she took off and shook her fur hat, if you had the bottle to
stand near. Belle had always worn hers long in a knot.
Johnny in a romper-suit, and that eedjit as usual getting
his own shadow in the picture, and her hair shining black
in the sun, the way she'd been holding her head.

'Did ye tell them ye was once a ballet-dancer?' chirped
Mrs Weston, peering over her shoulder.

'Whit the fuck use wad that be?'

'Ah, Mrs Smith!' The bright welfare voice, not too
delighted at the language. They hadn't heard her coming:
Belle jumped and shoved the photos guiltily inside her
coat. 'I haven't kept you waiting, have I?'

'I've nae other appointments,' said Belle sourly.

'Only the paper phoned to check the meeting-place. I
thought the park would be better than here. I mean – ' It
was a laugh to see her trying not to breathe in.

Belle scrambled to her feet without the offered hand.
Her beret just reached the neat tweed shoulder. 'Better'n
your fuck'n office,' she said.

They paused outside the park gate. Belle was trembling
so much she was afraid the nosy bitch would see. She
dragged the belt of her huge raincoat another notch tighter,
taking a long time over tucking in the loose end.

The welfare wumman said, quite gently for her, 'He

really wants to find you, Mrs Smith. That's why he put the
ad in the paper.'

'He'll maybe rue the day,' said Belle. She glared into the
concerned face above her. She said hardily, 'I'm gonny
stand up for my rights, so I am. I didny come up the Clyde
in a banana boat.'

The welfare wumman looked down at Belle. She seemed
a bit worried. 'I wish we'd allowed time to – '

'Clean me up?' snarled Belle.

They entered the park.

There were three men on the bench, but Belle wasn't in
any doubt. The reporter and photographer stood back
respectfully and Johnny got up. Still the blue eyes. Still
the pink face as well, a bit too pink and heavy. Need tae
watch that, son, that's the way yer daddy died.

'Mr Smith?' said the reporter eagerly.

Johnny hesitated. He's no' sure but he disny like to say
so. Well, admitted Belle tensely, there's maybe right enough
a wee bit change in me.

'Mrs Smith?' You would nearly think the wumman was
on Belle's side.

'I dunno – ' How the hell were ye supposed tae know him,
a fat young fella over thirty, last seen asleep in a blanket
and twenty-one months old? Bloody daft ye'd feel tellin'
the world he's got his daddy's eyes.

The reporter was just about wetting himself in his
excitement. 'The photos, the photos!'

'Yes – ' Johnny said, and took out his wallet. There it
was, the same back green; a slightly different pose, for
he'd called to them, laughing, to move away from the bin-
shelter this time; the same romper-suit, the same black-
haired young woman poised like a swan.

Belle shook with joy. She fumbled inside her coat and
held out her photograph, never taking her eyes off Johnny.
She couldn't read, at first, the expression that shaded his
determined plump pink smile.

He was staring so strangely at the photograph that she looked too, and saw the curly hair and chubby chops of the young Mrs Weston. She made to put her hand back inside her trollopy long raincoat, in among the ragged jerseys, to fish out the right photo. She stopped, because now she recognized it for what it was, the naked relief on Johnny's face.

Back at the archways she said, 'He wis a chancer that yin. I telt him whaur tae get aff. Wantin' a chape skivvy, ur ye, son? I gied him a sherrickin' he'll no' forget in a hurry.'

'Ye did right, Belle, so ye did,' sympathized Lizzie, false as hell.

'I telt ye there was hunners o' Isabella Smiths,' Belle said grimly. She began to drag the daytime rubbish out of her cardboard box.

Mrs Weston was really sympathetic, which was worse. 'You're surely no' turnin' in, Belle? It's hardly went twelve.'

'Ma back's killin' me,' said Belle. 'Never even offered me a sate.'

'Tae think,' sighed Mrs Weston. 'Yer allowance! Yer ain telly!'

'Here,' said Belle abruptly. 'I went aff wi' your photy.'

Sharp Lizzie said 'Ye didny show him that by mistake, did ye?'

'Aw, helluva funny,' said Belle. She removed her tiny cracked shoes and placed them neatly on the slimy cobbles, side by side. She crawled into her cardboard box and rolled herself up in her blanket, but she didn't sleep.

MATURITY

Kirkpatrick Dobie

He would have to go down. He would have to go down and face them. It would be his seventh descent and by far the steepest. When he arrived a week ago he had been surprised to find nothing but women. He had not cared for that and had said so but been assured they were elderly. 'As a rule I accept only people of good standing – professional people – teachers, solicitors, an occasional accountant – chartered of course.' That was what she had said and had made out he was an exception. But the previous night there had been these three unqualified girls – drama students on a weekend course. Gracious, Mrs Effingham might be – and she was his mother's cousin – but she was not a woman of principle.

Mary, Elizabeth, Rebecca – Stuart, Ackworth, Rosenberg. That was it. Scottish, English, Jewish, a mixed grill. He had a good memory for names but could not remember faces. He tended to ignore faces, especially women's. The girls had been talkative. They had even tried to involve him in their talk. So far as he could recall they were much about the same size and shape. There was nothing to go on.

Even before the girls it had been a bad week. The older women, regular residents each with privileged seat and corner, had tried to sift him and shown resentment when they failed. Not that it mattered. Appearances apart, he would have preferred to read at meals. As it was, he had addressed himself to interior thought, a discipline he had been practising for some time. The mind, according to Milton, was its own place. He agreed with that. When Mrs Effingham asked: 'What are you thinking of, David?' he

had at first affected not to hear, then answered with delib-
eration that it would take too long to tell her. It served
notice he did not mean to waste his time.

He had fixed on 'Though I speak with the tongues of
men and of angels'. Tongues, of course, were languages –
French, Latin, Greek, or for Paul, Greek, Hebrew,
Aramaic. These were tongues of men but what were
tongues of angels? It was something to think about. Then,
there were tongues of fire, the cloven tongues of Pentecost.
Could these be the tongues of angels? It seemed possible,
anyhow, worth considering. Best approach was Carlyle's
'Hold thy tongue! Thou hast it a-holding! Speak not, I
passionately beseech thee till thy thought shall have ma-
tured itself, till thou hast other than mad and mad-making
noises to emit.'

That his feeling concerning mad-making noises com-
municated itself was hardly his fault. He desired only to be
left alone. At twenty he had no small talk and no desire for
it. He recognized its place in a pastoral situation, but the
fact was his vocation did not lie there – 'Do all speak with
tongues? Do all interpret?'

He had tried and failed. There had been a man he met
often on Saturday mornings walking into town. Usually
they were on opposite sides of the road, too remote for
verbal greeting. He would have raised his hat could he have
caught the other's eye, but each time he tried, the man
looked away and he was left with an embarrassing half-
gesture. To break the deadlock he had one morning made
his attempt early, acting like a man shooting at geese who
aims ahead of the bird. The manoeuvre had been successful. The stranger's face had brightened but just as it did,
its owner kicked something on the pavement. He had not
exactly fallen but plunged headlong for yards before re-
covering himself. From then on, he averted his face, and
once when they happened to be on the same side, had
crossed the road.

But if he, David Penrose, did not have the common touch, he had something better – dedication. 'Cease this chaotic hub-bub in which thy whole soul runs to confused dislocation and waste!' That was Carlyle again and Carlyle too, had been designed for the ministry. He had left it only to address a wider audience.

But as he straightened his tie and took a last look at himself he thought Carlyle's struggles had at least been printable. There was no record of him as man or student waking in the night to find his bed invaded by a woman.

What followed had been unimaginable. He could not, even now, believe that anyone – any woman – could behave like it, or that he, resisting at first, could be drawn into such behaviour. It had left him drained and confused, in no condition to descend into that hen-house and sit there as if nothing had happened, not knowing which of these girls – for it must have been one of them – was his rapist.

Because he dared not be last to arrive – cynosure of all eyes, but especially of one pair, he descended quickly, found the place appointed him on his arrival, and having made some response to Mrs Effingham's bright good morning, was presently accepting cornflakes from the maid.

No one else greeted him but as he ate he began to feel better. It would be wise, he thought, to look and behave normally, perhaps even to talk. In conversation something might be revealed. On his left was Mrs Trumper, an archaeologist. She, of course, was old – too old. Had she worked in the Holy Land he enquired. Head down, mouth full, she replied: 'No! Far from it! The British Museum.'

At least it broke the ice. 'I ask', he said, 'because I am a student of divinity,' and he went on to speak of his studies, naming professors, referring to publications, but all the time aware of the girls – there were only two as yet down – wondering about the third, wondering if they were listening, hoping they were, and wondering too what they whispered. It could hardly be about last night. And yet, and yet, girls nowadays were as bad as boys. You had only to look at television.

Naturally, he absolved himself. He had been taken by surprise, been, in fact, asleep and so was blameless. He had, he decided, taken no consenting part. Best thing was to put it all out of mine. Indeed there was nothing else to do. It was not a thing to dwell on and to complain would only meet denial, perhaps ridicule. Perhaps that was what had been intended. Complaint, in any case, would reach his mother and he could not bear that. It would destroy his most precious relationship.

It could be the maid. Her bosom had touched his shoulder when she set down his plate. It might have no significance and she was, perhaps, a little heavy, though that did not rule her out. Then she was young, possibly sixteen, but girls of her class were old for their years. The whole thing was disgusting.

'This seems quite a comfortable house,' he said, addressing his righthand neighbour. She, at least, could be ruled out. Over sixty, she walked with a stick. 'Does Mrs Effingham have much help?'

The woman had stared. 'Two,' she said at last. 'A girl and a woman.'

'Ah! Only two? With cooking, cleaning, and all the rest of it, they must be kept busy. Do they live in?'

'How should I know? Do you want to sleep with them?'

He could hardly believe his ears. She had not even lowered her voice. 'Certainly not!' he heard himself hiss. 'I think you know very well what I intend to be my profession!'

'Nothing to me. I'm an anthropologist, you're a man. Desire is constant in the male – unless there's something wrong with him.'

'*I* am a Christian, not a wild beast!' and he turned his head away.

It was hard to tell how much of this had been overheard for at that moment the third girl appeared. Miss Ackworth, it seemed, had slept badly but before the admission could be assessed, the fact was confirmed by her room-mate. A room-mate, of course, proved nothing. The pair could be in collusion, and then, Miss Rosenberg would be Jewish. He had, of course, no prejudice against Jews but they were undeniably subtle. Anyhow, collusion or not, neither would be awake all night. What was certain was their weariness. Heavy with sleep, Miss Ackworth was eminently desirable. Before he could repudiate the idea someone was shouting: 'I understood you to say you were a Christian! I ask again, what you mean by it?'

This one was old too, sitting opposite, chin thrust out like a hungry pike, broad shoulders, powerfully built. The fact was, nobody could be excluded. Meredith, she was. Dr Meredith. Philosophy, he remembered. He eyed her angrily and it occurred to him he was getting better at eyeing people. That might be desperation but he was enjoying his breakfast too and that also was surprising. Ordinarily, he never noticed food. His mother was always pressing him to eat. 'I am Church of Scotland,' he said, and went on to explain what it meant.

It took some time and while at it his thoughts drifted to Miss Stuart. She must have slept by herself – if sleep she did. Anyhow, she must have had unrestricted opportunity. He glanced in her direction and found her glancing in his. He looked away.

'You study divinity? You aim to be a minister?'

'Yes.'

Dr Meredith, though grey-haired, was plump with pink cheeks.

'Yes,' he repeated. 'I could, of course, go into education. One is not confined to the pulpit.' Here he surprised himself. He had never before thought of education. Always it had been the pulpit. Much of his thought was given to preparing sermons.

'By education, you mean religious education?'

'Yes. The church has a department.'

'I find that strange. Not that the church has what you call a department, but that you, at your age, should feel competent to tell people how to order their lives. Old though I am, *I* should shrink from it. I shouldn't think I knew enough. *You* see no difficulty?'

Her words carried so much energy and implication that he hardly knew where to begin. Clearly, she was the type. And yet you could not go by words, or even by looks. It might, after all, be the maid.

He said: 'I do not make the rules. God has done that.'

They were all listening now but he didn't mind. He was doing well and felt perfectly relaxed. He helped himself to toast.

'And how do you know this?' The pink jaw thrust at him.

'I'm not sure I understand you.'

'Simple! You've certain rules – precepts – standards – I don't know what – and these, if I follow you, you mean to preach and practise. I ask how you arrive at them. Not from experience for you have little or none, so it's from something else. You say God, but all it is, is parents, teachers, or the Bible. You only mean you've accepted what you were told.'

He had not thought of his convictions like that. His mother, he saw now, had been their main source. It would, however, be unwise to say so.

'Of course,' the jaw went on, you may have had a personal revelation. They are not uncommon. A niece of mine had one. It occurred after she failed her finals. The difficulty is that by their nature such experiences are indistinguishable from mere assertion.'

43

'I believe,' he said, 'that I have responded to God's word.'

'The Bible?'

'Yes!'

'And how do you know it's God's word? It's full of discrepancies and contradiction. Barbarisms are recommended – see Psalm 137. I take it you don't intend to preach infanticide? If so, all you mean by responding to God's word is that you respond to your own judgement. I ask, what at your age is that worth?'

A terrible woman. Capable, clearly, of anything – especially anything aggressive – and plainly out to humiliate. But however ill-intentioned she was too large to be suspect. And yet again, there was no absolute certainty. It was impossible to say how she would appear undressed and in the dark. Who could tell how much would be taken off? Shoes were an example. They must add almost an inch. When he thought about it he realized that practically all women walked about on tiptoe. It was a revelation.

He had shaken himself. He had shaken his head. It had not been doubt or dismay. It had been a tremor but not timidity, rather the sort of shudder he had seen in the great horse attached to a neighbouring farm when once in a while men came with ropes to lead it away. 'What' he cried, 'do *you* know of my experience or judgement? At least I'm not such a fool as to confuse Christianity with the Old Testament!'

He had not waited for reply. He had raised his voice even more. 'Miss Stuart!' he had called to the other end of the table, 'tell me, did you sleep well? We have heard that one of your companions did not!'

She had been looking at him again, but it did not signify, for they had all been looking at him. Whether they liked it or not, he was their preoccupation. They could not help it. In that place, at that moment, he was master.

'Thanks! I slept quite well – when I *did* sleep.'

44

'So did I! So did I! Our experience has been the same –
or at any rate, similar.' She was, he thought, the prettiest
of the three.

'You are a drama student,' he went on. 'Do you intend
to act?'

He had nothing in mind. He wished only to prolong the
situation.

'Do *you*?' she asked. 'I mean, isn't preaching just
acting?'

'Of course! Of course! That's just what it is!' He felt as
if intoxicated. 'A service is just a show!' He rose to his feet.
'We do show the Lord's death till he come,' he said. 'It's
the greatest show on earth.'

He had them guessing. They didn't know where they
were – whether he was offended or had simply finished his
breakfast.

Mrs Effingham said: 'All the world's a stage, and all the
men and women merely players.'

The Meredith women croaked: 'I accept that – so long
as none of them try to play God.'

He bowed to her, paused, bowed again comprehensively,
bowed to Mrs Effingham and walked out. An effective exit.

Mrs Effingham said, 'I have written your mother and told
her I think we are too exclusively feminine for you, that
at your age you would be better in a mixed establishment.'

She was gracious, he thought, gracious but worldly,
neither old nor young, but mature – like those wicked
Edwardian ladies.

'Nevertheless,' Mrs Effingham went on, 'I think you
may have profited by your stay here, brief though it has
been.'

She wore scent and it stirred something in his too active
mind. He put the thought away. 'Perhaps you are right,'
he said. 'Though I think I should have liked to stay a little
longer.'

45

KRAKATOA, EAST OF JAVA

Maureen Duff

Never met the right man. Never had a child. It was running through her head like two streams of a river of soup. And she was crossing. Left, right, left, right. Among the breathing bodies she was the only one alive in the night.

It was almost funny. A broken arm? How could it have happened? It had all been such a surprise when she fell. She didn't remember a thing after the flash. They'd been kind enough, the ambulance men. One of them, the tall thin stooping one, had said 'Bones get brittle you know.' And he'd smiled and rubbed his nose. That had made her angry. She wanted to poke out his sympathy.

And then there was the young Nurse Andrews, calling her 'Nellie' if you please. All acne and no respect. Hardly more than a child. Well that had been a shock. In her day patients were the same age as the nurses. The doctors too. Some of them looked about twenty. Helen Jones was glum. How were you expected to feel right about it?

Doctor What's-his-name had scratched his beard and asked, 'How are you off at home, Miss Jones? Someone to look after you?' Hah. She'd looked after herself all this time, without anyone. How dare he suggest a broken arm would invalid her out of life. Why, she'd plenty of money in the bank, if she needed help.

Since she'd been wheeled into hospital in the afternoon, each minute had thrown up another insult like lava from a volcano. Krakatoa, that was a volcano run by the Japs, and the flash she knew had been something to do with the plug for the television set.

'Maybe you'd better have a word with Mrs Pagett.'

'Who's she?'

'Social work department.'

'Whatever for?'

'Meals on wheels.'

That did it. It was only three steps to the door and she'd be out. 'Miss Jones, where on earth are you going? The plaster hasn't set yet.' The doctor pressed his hands to her shoulders as she struggled to rise. Nice hands. Strong hands. How could she fight him? Something unravelled inside like soft spaghetti. But she heard her voice, spitting like a cat.

'Feed the cats. That's what old dears do, isn't it?'

'Can't you telephone a neighbour?'

'I've got ten of 'em.'

'Well, can't one of them. . . .'

'Cats.'

'Oh, I see.' The doctor shrugged. 'You must stay in for a few days. You've had a shock.'

But she couldn't look at him because he believed her. And one thing Helen Jones did not do was tell lies.

'I'll see if Mrs Pagett can send someone.'

'Hah. Mrs Pagett.'

She didn't know what else to say. So she said nothing and was wheeled back to Catherine Ward.

Now, in the dark, with the night lights burning, she was stiff and covered in dew. Ladies do not sweat, she informed herself. Sweating ladies never find the right man, said a voice. How stupid. She'd given up thinking about men years ago. In 1936 to be exact, on the tenth of April, at half past five in the afternoon. Oh why, why think of it at all. He had not been the right man.

She reached out with her good arm, the left one, and managed to knock a flood of water across the linoleum. She

47

lay there, thirsty, and for some unaccountable reason pleased with herself, while Nurse Andrews cleaned it up.

'Next time ask someone, will you, dear?'

Old lady, she thought, that's what they think I am. Who do they belong to, these children? I'd like to know so I can send 'em packing. She could feel her heart beating louder than ever. All sorts of thoughts shuffled inside like shifting sands. With astonishment she suddenly wondered if Arthur Simpson's bones were brittle too. And that was enough to send her pulse racing with hope.

Mrs Pagett was a tall woman with auburn hair and a flattish, almost horizontal brow. She reminded Helen Jones of a red setter.

'Cats. That's the problem.' A smile with grey fillings. Helen nodded. 'Well, there's a simple solution. If you would like to give me your keys, we'll send someone round to feed them for you. Nurse Andrews' mother lives in the next street and she has kindly offered. . . .'

Helen's head was shaking uncontrollably. This was an outrage. A violation. Mrs Pagett coloured. She flicked open the notebook on her lap.

'Now Miss Jones, unless somebody goes in, your pussies will starve, will they not?'

'Hah.'

'Are you being difficult Miss Jones?' Mrs Pagett's pencil point snapped on the notebook. Snap was a game, thought Helen, and stared at Mrs Pagett's hands. They were covered in freckles.

'Miss Jones, please pay attention to what I am saying. I have another appointment.'

But Helen was aware only of freckles. Her own mother had freckles all over her body. In the summer her arms were roses and gold, blooming among her favourite blue and white cotton frock.

Oh, the frocks in Adams Wood. On the day of the picnic her mother's sisters' frocks were like pillows you could

48

rest your head upon. And all the men had beards, like the young doctor. Boys trying to be men, striding out to keep up with the excited girls, while the women sailed behind with the picnic baskets. Oh and there was Arthur Simpson with his flat cap like one of the work boys from the village, running away from everyone, through a tunnel of green leaves into the darkest part of the wood. He always wore his cap so it covered the bald spot on his crown. And everybody teased him. Helen Jones was suddenly overcome with a desire to weep, and to punch the Pagett woman at the same time.

'The cats can starve,' she said and stared out of the window. She was finished with Pagett.

'Now Miss Jones, really.' Mrs Pagett tore a page from her notebook and screwed it up.

Brittle, thought Helen Jones, Pagett was brittle. There would be no tears for the Pagett.

'Well, it's up to you. I'll get Doctor to have a word with you about it later.'

Mrs Pagett's voice reached Helen from the end of a tunnel. And what connected Helen to the brightness was the angle of pain from shoulder to wrist, all wrapped up like a Christmas present in hard packed snow and ice, while the rest of Helen crouched softly inside her and tried to make sense of the rivers of soup. She had to remember it exactly. She had to find out where it hurt. And it was in the wood.

Arthur Simpson's cap had come off beyond the stream in the dark of the wood. He'd taken it off and leant against a tree. Then a branch had snapped and he'd found her hiding there, watching him.

'I was not.'

'Yes you were. You're a hussy.'

That was the word. He wouldn't see her turn red in this dark. So she said, 'Am not.' But she was hot.

And he said ever so softly so she could hardly hear,

'Nellie Jones is a pure little tart.'

There, that was it. That was what he'd said.

Now it didn't hurt so badly to say it, now did it, did it? Only a bad man would say such a thing to a young girl. Arthur Simpson's chest was magnificent, but he was a bad man. But what if it was just words? What if he'd not meant it at all? If it was a joke? Would that have made it all right? When he put his cap back on and pushed her down, he tried to kiss her, and then didn't.

Helen Jones of the bright light whimpered and demanded water from Nurse Andrews. And it came with a straw which was bent in the middle. And that was a relief because she could not, in the middle of the morning, sit up at all.

'There we are, dear. Doctor'll be round soon.'

The one with the beard, no doubt.

The beard, whispered the darkness. And it was there, making her face redder, but it was all right as long as he didn't kiss her mouth. That's what they'd told her, the village girls. He kissed everything else though.

'You're hot,' he said. 'Sweating like a tart.'

'I don't sweat.'

'Well you're wet all over, Nellie Jones. What'll your mam say about that then?'

'Oh.' She didn't dare think.

'She'll have powder all over you, now won't she? Like here. And here. And up here.'

And his hands were all in places they shouldn't be.

'You get off me, Arthur Simpson, or I'll tell my mam.'

'She'll be jealous then, won't she. Oh, stop moving will you.'

'I'm too scared.'

'I won't hurt you. You just put your hand on that, and ...'

'Oh.'

'... easy now, just keep still ...'

'But what if anything happens, you know ...'

'I won't hurt you Nellie.'

'Oh, right.' For she was brave, but there were ants in the ground. She could feel them running everywhere out of the roots of the trees and over her bare legs. And still he had his cap on as he moved inside her, again and again. And the pain was different. Not what they'd said. She loved it, loved it. Anyway what was she supposed to do? She was trapped by his magnificent chest, and her rising fear of a child, and what he would think of her. She wasn't a tart. She just liked her nails sliding and scratching on the back of this sweating man who was so bad and strong. What was wrong with it? He could shout at her mam, louder than her mam, and then he shouted and roared through his beard, oh delicious, shocking roars. . . .

'I love you Nellie YOU LITTLE BITCH!'

YOU FILTHY LITTLE BITCH.

Of all the stupid things. Another snap. This time of anger flowing through the branches, through the green-stained wood, a clout of anger raised in a scream. The blue and white frock covered the sky and her mam, her mam, stood screaming out her rage.

OH HE *WAS* A BAD MAN. He ran away and left his cap behind. That was how scared he was of her mam. And he left her to drink it all in. The dead roses. The dull gold.

And yes he did it all. And no he didn't touch me, Mam. And if you say so anything. He made me do it. How I struggled but his chest held me down. And he didn't let me speak. He kept kissing me, Mam, I couldn't shout. It's not my fault.

And then just staring open-mouthed at her mam's rage which didn't stop, till it screamed inside her own head and belonged to her for ever. Mine all mine. And her mam looked pleased and became quiet and folded up the knickers and went away into the cold blue and white sky. Helen dragged behind, all wet. She was hot and shivered in the wind. Later she was washed and powdered like a child.

Arthur Simpson ran away to the South China Seas. He must have hated her. But not as much as she hated him.

And when she remembered the hairs on his chest, she shivered.

Helen shut her eyes and the tears ran down the inside of her face. The longer they stood in the doorway of the shop the longer she would wait. The more the pain in her legs came the more she would not give in. It was a game she'd learned that went on and on till someone said snap. And every time she won. This time there were three of them. A brother and two sisters, cousins of Arthur Simpson. They were watching her, curious to see if she were – mad? Well, she would show them she was *not* peculiar.

'What's it like then, Nellie?'

She was hot down her spine. Weak with shame and rage.

'I don't know what you mean.'

'Don't touch her or you'll die.'

I'm a fragile China doll, whispered dark Helen, but I won't break. She waited and watched till the tears were safely dried inside.

'Put stones down her neck.'

But still she did not break in the rush of pebbles to her spine. Her nails bit into the palms of her hands. She stood till she was cold and full of shivers. And then they let her pass because they were afraid of her silence which went on and on.

'Why are you so late?'

Mam's voice was *that* way again as if her throat were tied with string. 'The bus broke down. I had to walk from the village.'

And Helen crept before the fire which cracked and sang. And she smiled as she roasted in the shower of sparks. She was hot, but oh she was a lady and ladies do not sweat. And the shivers vanished to the end of a tunnel, like smoke in the chimney.

'You haven't been . . .'

'No, Mam.' The shaking was a China saucer somewhere behind the ribs. To stop it breaking, breathe out and whisper, 'No, the bus broke down. I don't tell lies.'

Mam's not sure. But oh, isn't she beautiful, shaking coal from the scuttle on to the fire, making the sparks fly, with her smooth hair pulled back, streaked with red lights. The roses and the gold were shining in the fire and then there was a turning and a satisfied smile. 'Well, after you've eaten your dinner, it's time to write that letter, like a good girl.'

And as Mam put out the dinner, Helen was so sleepy and safe she knew it was for the best. There was only the curious shaking in her hands that caused a saucer to tumble to the floor. But it didn't break. And the shaking belonged to someone else who lived at the end of a tunnel. And Mam smiled again.

And Helen smiled. 'Mam, will you tell me what to write?'

'Do you remember what happened?' A masculine voice, like velvet. Helen Jones shook her head, and dared to look. The brown-eyed one. The bearded one.

'You said something about a television set yesterday.'

'Hm. It was the plug.'

'That's how you got the shock?'

'No it stopped the volcano. You know, Krakatoa. The Japs.'

The doctor sat down by the bed. Helen watched the expression on his face, through the beard. He thought she was daft.

'I was trying to blow myself up if you must know.'

The doctor was silent for a moment. Then he sighed and leaned forward. 'Mrs Pagett said you wouldn't give her the key to your flat.'

Bright Helen said 'Hah.' And dark Helen crouched nearer, and stretched her neck towards him.

And then he pounced on the cold ice parcel, and bright Helen yelled out. 'It's all right, Miss Jones, I haven't touched you. Now tell me where it hurts exactly.'

And he took her hand, her good hand, and held it firmly, while dark Helen gasped and wondered about him. She looked at the hairs on his strong arms. And at his back curving over her. Taking her pulse, and holding her by her tiny white wrist.

And Helen breathed out and in as he asked her, while the stethoscope searched her body and she became sleepy while he murmured on.

She could listen to him for ever, and the pain in her arm was somehow far away at the end of a tunnel. Then there was a smile, and he said, 'Would you give *me* the key, Miss Jones?'

Helen watched and waited and he slipped his hand into her locker and emerged with the key. She would have told him then there were no cats but he didn't ask.

Tell him, whispered a voice at the end of the tunnel. She was coming nearer, that dark girl who was so stupid and shivering.

Tell him about Krakatoa. Arthur sent you postcards.

No he was a bad man.

He wanted you to write.

I did write.

You wrote him lies. You told him there was a child called Nellie.

There was *a child.*

But it died before its time.

No, no. Its name was Helen.

He sent you money for the child. Every month for six years.

Mam knew he was a bad man. She said he had to pay.

But when he wanted to come back for you, why didn't you tell him then there was no child?

Mam said he wouldn't come. And she was right.

He said he was coming anyway, when his cousins told him there was no child.

Well he didn't come, did he? He was drowned by the Japs.

The merchant seaman in the war was only missing . . .
Perhaps he's still in Singapore, the captain of a cutter . . .

No, no. He must be dead. The money stopped.

. . . Arthur Simpson with a fine grey beard, and brittle
bones and a laugh that would frighten the dead . . .

He'd only have wanted the money back.

. . . and Mam is dead.

And silence wandered through the mind of Helen Jones.
Between the far-off stream and the stringy dryness in her
throat was what? In the wheels of a hospital trolley, she
heard only the far-off rumble of a volcano.

'IT'S TOO LATE,' she said out loud in anger. 'HE'S
GONE TO THE BOTTOM OF THE SEA.' The doctor
looked round puzzled and looked away.

And dark Helen whispered from her tunnel. . . . Tell this
man there are no cats.

He was moving away to another bed, in slow motion.

Dark Helen pulled on the wrapping of the cold white
parcel, and the pain was sharp. Do it, do it now. And bright
Helen breathed deeply. She had such a little voice.

'Doctor I want to tell you . . .'

Doctor Pagett your wife is on the phone. Nurse Andrews
trotted into the ward and trotted out again. And the world
flashed, and rumbled and snapped in two. And dark Helen
was a speck at the end of a tunnel which had once led to
somewhere. A tidal wave splashed through the past and
Helen Jones rose brittle into the bright world for ever.

'Yes, Miss Jones?'

'I just wanted to tell you doctor, that I've got fifty
elephants and three blind mice as well as the cats, so you
can tell that red setter wife of yours to keep her wet nose
out of my affairs, unless she can provide meals on wheels
for the lot. Now pass me that tin of powder will you. I'm
a little hot.'

And Helen Jones sank back on to the blue and white
pillows and thought no more of Krakatoa, East of Java.

MOSSY

Audrey Evans

Miss Stone had her departure from the school nicely planned. At one minute to four, she lined them up. Ten seconds before the bell, she sent a boy to spit his bubble-gum into the wastepaper basket. Then she dismissed her very last class. They walked demurely down the corridor, then roared off round the corner. Miss Stone, a complacent smile on her neat, blunt features, picked up her coat and briefcase, and nipped across the corridor into the Detention Room.

There, studying the Detention Book, was Mr Downie, youngest and newest teacher on the Staff.

'Mr Downie,' she said. He jumped, and Miss Stone smiled grimly.

'As you know, I retired from teaching at 4 pm today.'

Mr Downie appeared to be at a loss.

'You're not having a party, then?' he said.

'Certainly not. The Rector being unctuous, concealing how much we dislike each other; other members of the staff who were once pupils here – an incestuous situation, don't you think? – would recall how I once belted them. No thank you. Now, I would like – '

'I was once a pupil here,' said Mr Downie, 'and you belted me.'

'Indeed? I didn't realize. But then I have never involved myself with my former pupils.'

'You weren't much interested in your current ones.'

Miss Stone's eyebrows rose. Mr Downie was evidently made bold by the prospect of her departure.

'I'm sorry I haven't time for a stroll down Memory Lane,' she said. 'I have a favour to ask of you. If you would be so good – '

'If I would be so good! Always the soul of courtesy, you were. Till there was trouble. Then it was a hand like a breeze block rearranging your brains. I think you impaired my hearing permanently.'

'Then I must speak louder. I would like to take your Detention, this evening.'

There was a bewildered silence.

'You mean do my Friday night Detention for me?'

Miss Stone sighed and waited.

'Why? I mean . . . I've been lumbered with it all term, and nobody's ever agreed to swop with me. Who would? Dammit, it's Friday, isn't it? And,' he went on, marvelling, 'you wouldn't be swopping if you're leaving today – '

'Mr Downie,' said Miss Stone, losing patience, 'I wish to avoid certain contingencies. Such as the medium sweet sherry, now awaiting me as a surprise in the Ladies' Staff Room. Another is having my hand shaken warmly by colleagues whom I have detested for years. In short, I want to hide until everybody has gone home. Will you assist me?'

Mr Downie grinned broadly.

'You should have been called Stony, not Mossy,' he said. 'You always had your own way, didn't you? I wish I had the knack. The kids terrify me.' He glanced down at the Detention Book and shuddered. 'Especially the girls. One thing I always appreciate, though – your sardonic sense of humour.' His own humour overcame him. 'OK, sister,' he said, 'you talked me into it.'

Miss Stone waited, looking down her nose.

'Yes, yes, thank you. I'll do it,' he said, his hand furtively covering his ear.

Left alone, Miss Stone settled at the teacher's desk, and had a look at the Detention Book. Only two names. She set her briefcase on the desk and opened it. Then her face went blank. It was a shock, slight but cutting, to realize that she had no correction to do. She liked to have work in hand when she was supervizing a class. Then, if there was any disturbance, she could look up, severe and preoccupied. It gave her, she felt, an advantage.

She sat, red pen tapping the desk, surveying the little room, designed to depress further pupils who were already in disgrace; from beige walls to buff ceiling and brown floor. It was like sitting inside a parcel.

Outside, in the corridor were footsteps and voices, and the harsh, dangerous shouts of boys. They gradually died away. She wished with a fervour that surprised her, that somebody would come in.

The door opened, and a small, very dirty boy edged round it. He came and stood at the desk. He didn't look round the room or at Miss Stone. In fact, he gave the impression of not looking anywhere. His eyes were as blank as marbles.

'You're . . . let me see . . . Wayne. Is that right?'

'Aye.'

'Here's your work.'

She handed him a booklet and a sheet of paper, and he wandered off to a seat. He took some time to settle, pulling out a pen, then a pencil, and looking at them as if he had no idea what to do with them. Then he opened the booklet and began to write, slowly and carefully, squinting along the paper, his head lying along his arm.

The door burst open. The girl's face sagged in disappointment when she saw who was sitting at the teacher's desk.

'Aw!' she said. 'Mossy! I mean – sorry, Miss Stone. Where's Mr Downie?'

'I am taking Detention tonight,' said Miss Stone, in her colourless voice.

'But Mr Downie – he always takes it on Friday.'

'Looking forward to seeing him, were you? I see it was he who set you the Detention. Sit down, please.'

The girl slumped into a seat. She was about fifteen, pretty in a heavy, moist sort of way. The boy, Wayne, had not raised his head, but wrote steadily on. The girl's flushed face looked as if it might turn resentful and truculent. Miss Stone moved in, with the ease of long practice.

'What is your name? Ah, yes. Dawn. So, Dawn, you made yourself obnoxious in Mr Downie's class. He gave you Detention. And you were hoping to be alone at last with him, give or take one or two other numbskulls, was that it? Well, I am sorry to disappoint you. Mr Downie wished to see his fiancée this evening, and I agreed to take his place.'

'Fiancée!' The foolish mouth dropped, the eyes filled with tears. Dawn took the sheet of paper and sat, blinking and sniffing, making no effort to write.

'Go on,' said Miss Stone. 'A 500-word essay on Good Manners. And mind you write in paragraphs.'

Miss Stone sat, erect yet relaxed, hands clasped in front of her. She felt as she usually did, completely in control of the classroom situation. Then she was annoyed to realize that she was consciously achieving that control by an effort. 'For goodness' sake,' she said to herself, 'what's the matter with you? Another half hour and you can send them home. Then you can get away, as you planned.' She thought of her austerely comfortable little flat, and the glass of fine dry sherry she had promised herself.

It was no good. She was rattled. Why? It wasn't that silly girl, now sighing heavily as she considered the concept of Good Manners. No. It was the boy. There was something incongruous in the contrast between his dirty clothes and close cropped hair, his plastic jacket and heavy laced boots, and his earnest, scribe-like endeavours.

She went over to him. He laboured on, entirely absorbed in his work. He was copying from a booklet called *Spelling*

for Primary Schools. There were lists of short, easy words
. . . 'able, ache, adder, affair'. His writing began large and
ungainly, then trailed uncertainly upwards. Some of the
words were wrongly spelt. She looked hard at the boy.

'What class are you in, Wayne?'

'2B Special, Miss.'

'How old are you?'

'Fourteen, Miss.'

She picked up his paper.

'Let me have a look. Good. That's very good, Wayne.
"April" has a capital letter, though.'

'Oh, aye,' said Wayne, and resumed his task.

'How many of these are you supposed to do?'

'Fifty.'

'You've done far more than that. You can stop now. I'll
put your work on the desk for Mr Price. He'll be pleased
with you.'

She put out her hand for the piece of paper. To her surprise, he snatched it up and held it to him.

'I want tae dae mair words,' he said.

'No, no.' She was patient, in an impersonal way, because
he was one of Mr Price's lot, in 2B Special. 'You've done
enough.'

She stood, waiting for him to obey, but he sat, head bent,
clutching the creased sheet of paper.

'Can I no dae mair words?'

Miss Stone was silent, puzzled.

'I like daen them!' His voice was suddenly loud and
rough with defiance, and Dawn glanced up.

'I can dae it. You said I was daen it guid. I'm guid at it.'

He laid his paper on the desk, and smoothed it out.

Miss Stone opened her mouth to say something so
sarcastic that it would sweep Wayne and his spelling list
out of the Detention Room and out of her life for ever. But
she did nothing of the kind. It was as if a veil had been
wrenched aside, and a hard clear light shone on this dirty

little boy. For the first time, in the long, cold years, she understood something . . . what he was saying . . . what he was telling her . . . why he was clinging to his pathetic task, so awkwardly done . . . that he was finding peace and satisfaction in the work. He was happy that he could cope. Everything in his school life was a fog of misunderstandings, a jungle of blundering errors, with no track to follow. Here, with his little book and his sheet of paper, he was like everybody else, successful and safe.

The moment of vision, with its pity, passed. To reassure herself, Miss Stone said, with a shaky laugh, 'You're not supposed to enjoy Detention, Wayne. You'll undermine the whole system.'

He sat silent, accepting yet again that he never knew what teachers meant.

Then he said, 'It's guid, this.' He gave a strong shiver. 'It's fine and warm, here. Quiet.'

He wiped his nose on his sleeve and began to write again.

Miss Stone became aware that Dawn was staring, mouth half open. She knew, by pupil instinct, that a teacher had lost control of a situation.

Miss Stone decided to get rid of her.

'Have you finished, Dawn?' she said.

'Here, no Miss,' said Dawn, startled.

Miss Stone went to look over her shoulder.

'It'll do,' she said. 'You can finish it next Friday, when Mr Downie's here. I'll make a note of it in the Detention Book.'

'Oh, great.' Dawn got to her feet. Then her face darkened. 'I didna know that Mr Downie was engaged.'

'Did I say that? I must have been mistaken.'

'He's not engaged?'

'Not at all. He is, in fact, still looking for his ideal woman. Better luck next Friday, Dawn.'

She watched the girl making ready to go, clumsy and

excited, like a puppy. She felt amused contempt for her, and an admiring awareness of her own malice and her . . . what had Mr Downie called it? . . . her sardonic humour.

At the door, the girl turned. She smiled radiantly, her face lit with love and joy.

'Thanks, Miss,' she said. 'You're great.'

Miss Stone felt that her moment of self-congratulation had been quite spoiled.

Left with Wayne, Miss Stone prowled round the Detention Room. While this wretched child was doing his Detention so conscientiously, *her* professional conscience directed that she should wait a little longer, even though all sound had died in the corridor and the Staff Room sherry would be long re-corked.

She glanced again at the Detention Sheet. Docherty . . . Docherty . . . a boy with the same shape of head and the same bristly fair hair.

'There was a Kevin Docherty,' she said.

Wayne jerked upright, and the pencil fell from his hand.

'That was my Dad, Miss,' he said.

'Miss What?' said Miss Stone, from force of habit.

'Miss Mossy.'

She shot a keen glance at him. Too stupid to be trying it on. He didn't look cocky; in fact, he was watching her almost as if he were frightened. Then his glance slid sideways.

'You tellt my Dad once he was as thick as a dry stane dyke.'

'Did I? I must have been annoyed with him. What's he doing these days?'

'Nothing,' said Wayne. He hesitated, blinking rapidly, then said, 'My Mam was in that class.'

'Oh? What was her name?'

'Janet.'

'What was her maiden name?'

Wayne looked blank.

'Her name before she married your Dad.' Wayne shook his head.

'Janet,' mused Miss Stone, '. . . Janet Stewart . . . That would be it, eh?'

'Dinna ken,' said Wayne.

'That would be in 1970. No, no, that would mean that Janet was only fifteen – ' She stopped, embarrassed. There was no reaction from Wayne. He picked up his pencil ready to start that interminable copying.

'Have you any brothers or sisters, Wayne?'

'Twa brithers. Twa sisters.' He began to write again.

Miss Stone reflected on Wayne's parents. Although she always claimed she couldn't remember a thing about her ex-pupils, she had excellent recall. Janet Stewart, a wee fair girl, and Kevin Docherty . . . She remembered him all right. Big hands curled into fists, blue eyes congested with sullen hatred, while she stood over him, raking him with a sarcasm against which he had no defence except whispered obscenities. She had beaten him under, but only just. One of those boys whose violent fate has been decided and who are destined to decide the fate of others. Poor, silly wee Janet. Fifteen years old. She hadn't stood a chance. Miss Stone shrugged off Janet and her like.

'Your father was a bit of a hard man when he was at school. Did you know that?'

'Aye,' said Wayne. Then he whispered, 'He batters me. And my Mam.'

Miss Stone recoiled in alarm and distaste. Serve her right for showing interest. It was time the boy went home.

'Wayne, you've done two whole sides. Now, off you go.'

He didn't move. Sitting on the edge of her desk, her patient tone becoming ragged, Miss Stone said, 'Wayne, look, this has been my last day in this school. I don't teach here any more. I want to go home. And you must go home, too.' She took the booklet and paper from him and placed them on the desk. He watched her, picking at a filthy thumbnail. With a return of that eerie clarity of vision, she saw how white his face was, how hollowed his eyes.

'Get rid of him,' she thought. 'He's trouble. Don't ask him any more questions. You're on your way home . . . get him and yourself out of this room, out of this school . . .'

It was too late.

'I canna go hame. I'm feart. I want to stay here.'

Dreading the answer, Miss Stone had to ask.

'Why are you afraid?'

'It's my Dad.'

It took ten full minutes to get the story out of him. At the end of it, Miss Stone sat back, appalled.

The father had beaten the boy and his mother repeatedly. The other children were in care. Last night, things had been very bad. The woman and child had crouched in the kitchen, listening to Docherty in his drunken frenzy, raging above them. In the morning they had crept about, thinking them-selves safe for a while. Then Wayne's father had flung open the kitchen door. The heavy, thudding blows on his mother had driven the boy beyond reason. He had picked up a heavy iron coal-shovel and struck at his father.

'It didna hurt him. It didna! Just his back. But he came at me and he said, "I'll kill you." An' I ran awa, an' he shouted after me, "When you come back the nicht, I'll batter you senseless! I'll kill you!" I was feart to go back. . . . I cam tae the school.'

'And you haven't told anyone about this? A teacher?'

'Naw. Just you, Miss.'

Just her. Miss Stone sprang to the Detention Room door and looked the length of the corridor. No one in sight. No one to help. Everyone had done what she had wanted them to do, and gone home, leaving her with a boy, who had gone through a whole school day, half out of his mind with terror at what lay in wait for him at the hands of his father.

'Mam,' said Wayne behind her, 'My Mam . . .'

It was growing cold in the Detention Room. Outside, it

was darkening, the wind was getting up, and rain was flung against the windows. Distracted, she muttered, 'The police – we could tell them – '

The boy started up in terror.

'No' the police!'

'But somebody must be told – '

Wayne's grimy hand clutched her arm, and even then she shuddered with distaste, because no child had ever dared touch her.

'No,' said Wayne. 'You come wi' me.'

'Come with you? Come with you where?'

'Hame. I'll no be feart if you come wi' me. Please. Please, Miss Mossy.'

Miss Stone pulled her arm free, and went to sit at the teacher's desk. She sat erect, as she had always done, contained and in command. But it was an outward show, a parody. Within her raged tempests of fear and anger.

'It's not fair,' she moaned. 'I've retired . . . I've escaped . . . it's nothing to do with me . . . Why should it be me? I've survived everything because I never *never* got involved – '

The boy stood anxious, at her shoulder, and for a moment she thought she must have cried aloud.

'Come on,' he said, and his face was old with dread.

Miss Stone was beaten at last. Defeated by the enemies she had held at bay so long: pity, and stronger by far, compassion.

She got up, her movements random and slow.

'Where do you live, Wayne?'

'The Valley.'

'Of course,' said Miss Stone, drearily. 'Where else?' Hay Valley Gardens, that septic patch of decaying warrens.

They walked along the corridor. Once, Miss Stone stumbled and nearly fell, for no reason.

'What will I find? Oh, what will I find?' Her mind threw up ranging images of fear and disgust. Kevin Docherty,

his great granite hands, his face full of an old hatred . . .
and a weeping, beaten woman. Sordid, violent, ugly
beyond belief . . . Among the terrors of what was to come,
there sounded, as from another world, the voice of Mr
Downie.

'I wish I had your sardonic sense of humour . . . you
always got your own way . . .'

Wayne looked up into her face.

'You're no' laughin' are you?'

'No. No. Not laughing.'

He put his hard, dirty little claw into her hand. She
closed her fingers strongly over it, but it was the boy who
drew *her* out into the rain and the wind and the dark.

THE BOARD OF GOVERNORS
OF THE HOUSE OF CHARITY

Patrick Farnon

I wouldn't dwell on her, wouldn't even think of her, the old bitch, if she didn't keep coming back unsolicited in the fragmented kind of dreams I have in the quiet of the afternoons sometimes and if it hadn't been for the fact, in the first place, that all of us children in the home couldn't help wondering about the book she kept in her desk giving the exact moment of our births, the state of the weather on the day, the position of the stars, the names of each of our parents with a full description of what they liked and what they didn't like, signed by their own hand on the cracked birth certificates rolled into a bundle in another, lower drawer of the desk behind which the matron sat; the certificates with the signatures scrawled in a colour never seen since between purple and black with a trace of necrotic green because the way they mixed colours in those days was different.

And with the door closed so that no one could disturb them, she and the reverend, who never took off his black shiny coat even in the hottest weather but only his dark hat, would sit with the book on the desk between them, he with his legs tightly crossed, one palm clasping the other and she with her thighs splayed, stretching her skirts to the limit, taut as sailcloth, her feet turned in, resting on their sides, showing the soles of her brogues, white as the tongues of sick cows; each of them taking a turn to tap the open pages with a finger, nodding just enough to swill their brains and their eyes in the fluid of their skulls, the matron's elbow adjacent to the black phone that never rang, its cord frayed where it entered the device, revealing a bright trace of red wiring that burned and twisted its way across the floor into the white porcelain socket set low on the wall at the other side.

Everything they knew about us they kept to themselves, even the things that went back to before the entries in the book and it was this knowledge, or lack of it, that commandeered a place in the morning and afternoon breaks and at the weekends too when we were permitted to go up the long stony avenue, between the trees that were supposed to be poplars, mindful of the repeated warnings not to speak with a single stranger in the village, let alone look at anyone.

But the real reason they didn't speak in that room, didn't need to, was that they had already decided what was to be done about all of us, what was to become of every single one since the day we were born and it was only when the straight-backed chair with its leather seat, smooth and bald as a drowned dog's pelt, became too much for the reverend's skinny back that he took the trouble to move his body and detach his legs and amble, hands clutched behind back, to challenge the attraction exercised by the dark oak panels that skirted the wall to half its height, and above the mitred frieze, ponder the oil painting, cracked as a mud-flat in mid-summer, of the Board of Governors of the House of Charity, while the matron selected a cheroot from the battered silver box and holding it between two stubby fingers, sucked it to her lips, her tongue curved round the stem, her other hand resting firmly on the desk to resist the temptation in the reverend's presence, to stroke, to caress at length her arms or her thighs or touch her face·or pluck at the mole on her cheek or finger the fine dark hairs on her upper lip.

And all the time she sat there, the smoke spreading flat along the ceiling, the reverend, pursing his lips, would pause on the centre of the paper-thin Persian carpet, immaculately swept, that contained the two chairs, the desk, the telephone, the smoke, the walls, the panels, the entire structure and everyone in it, including the servants, quick as ghosts in the long corridors of the grey-stone building of the House of Charity.

And if it hadn't been that I found out eventually what was going on they would have stayed like that forever, making up our thoughts because no one could stop them or wanted to, inventing them to wake us in the middle of the night in our two-tiered bunks in the dormitory, the moist sweat of escape on our foreheads, to half-witness a face at the window beckoning us from sleep and, when we opened our eyes, to be offered only the merciful tappings of the black night branches of the trees against the window panes.

Whether I was elected or not to put an end to it doesn't matter, but one day the matron had me summoned to her office and without preliminaries, merely with her hand flat on the desk-top holding down a sheet of paper and her gaze unflinching, informed me bluntly, 'You're a foundling.'

And as if there might be some doubt as to what that meant, she said,

'You were found. On a doorstep. In the village.'

And while I was thinking 'you, you' as if I were anyone at all, as if I were no one, afraid at the same time to look down to see whether the 'hooves', as Brother Bartholemew had called them, had brought in mud onto the carpet from the flower beds and the vegetable garden where I had just been I held my gaze on the hand, the paper and the bottom button of the matron's cardigan, respectful of that first occasion alone in her presence, as she continued all the while in a warning tone,

'There's no point in doing what the others do and trying to find out, because that won't do you any good. No good at all.'

All it would achieve was harm, she said, because they could have been anyone, my parents, a couple of gypsies, hop-pickers down for the season. Anyone. She was only saying it for my own good.

And because I was only about eight at the time I believed her every word and took the news quite philosophically back to where two companions of mine – Kane and Douglas – were flapping their legs on the playground wall, waiting for my return so that Kane could blurt out first as he always did, unable to suppress his curiosity,

'What did she say?'

I said that I had been lost and then I was found and they'd brought me here. But all Kane said was 'Oh' as if what he really meant was 'Me too' but suspecting how bad the truth might be he didn't want to believe it, in the same way as Douglas who had converted his attention to the tapping of his right heel against the wall.

So I kept my thoughts to myself till I was about twelve or thirteen, which was when the matron paid a visit to the dormitory just after the six o'clock bell and our pyjamas smelled of rancid sleep. She singled out about half-a-dozen of us, saying, 'you, you, you and you' and said she had good news and for us to wait before going down to breakfast. And when the others had filtered out to the cold wash-rooms, throwing us envious glances despite the early hour, she handed each a sealed envelope with no stamp – nothing, not even an address to indicate where it had come from, and told us to open it at our convenience, by which she meant not in her presence, which is one of the reasons I was never witness to what the rest found in theirs. I waited till the toilets were vacated, first taking the precaution of standing on the bowl and peering over the partition into the adjacent cubicles to make sure they were empty. I took out the note that was inside the envelope. At first it meant nothing to me, Jeremiah Francis Thigglewaite, because I had never heard such names before, not all three together, not like that, one behind the other in that order as if they naturally belonged together. And it was only when a surge of joy passed through me I knew they were my names from now on, my official title to be spoken with respect on everyone's lips. No longer would I have 'Ali Wong' called after me because I wore an orange-coloured suit of inch-thick tweed that came in a brown-paper charity parcel tied with hairy string and I had a pointed head and cropped sandy hair and eyebrows white as a rabbit's and looked like no one else on earth.

So I crumpled the envelope into a ball and giving the chain two powerful tugs to make doubly certain, flushed it roaring down the drain and kept the note to take it out in the ensuing weeks at every conceivable opportunity, to study or just to glance at and fold up again. I kept it in the top pocket of my jacket, then in the rear pocket of my long, baggy trousers and sometimes hidden inside, in the torn lining, or folded up very small in the tiny pocket on the other side and for weeks afterwards I hung around the corridors and the classrooms, my eyes moist, hoping to ambush the matron in her heavy skirts that carried her body about the school and under which her legs moved, because I planned secretly to throw myself at her and kiss the hems of her skirts, impress my lips on her dull shoes in the manner demonstrated by noble persons in our history books, because that was the only way I was capable of imagining the expression of gratitude between one person and another, then.

But she didn't turn up and it was just afterwards that I was requested to use my new names for the first time on the annual examination paper in the great hall presided over by Brother Bartholemew, who had contact with God, wore a gold watch with a gold bracelet on his wrist and was the reverend's assistant as far as *we* understood. He told us to write our name in full at the top of the paper and then holding up his wrist to look the gold watch in the face to tell us it was not yet time to start the examination, said the whole purpose of the thing was to decide what we would become later in life.

I recall that distinctly. 'Later in life,' he said, and the word 'life' combined with the euphoria of using my new name for the first time in the open sent such a shiver down my spine, into my stomach, that shamefully I had to request permission to leave the hall and when I returned the exam was already under way. I could do no more than stare miserably at the three words at the top of the sheet, Jeremiah Francis Thigglewaite, the number of the class and the date, all neatly underlined and held up by a block of unnatural white, till the bell rang to indicate it was all over for another year.

And although the suspicion was beginning to filter through then that I'd received these names only for the purpose of scratching them on that ignominious document, the process of disillusion was lengthy and full disappointment kept long in abeyance by the great excitement of being already famous.

I practised my names everywhere. At night in the dormitory I pulled the musty brown woollen blankets over my head and wrote them out in full – laboriously at first, then with increasing ease, filling notebook after notebook, and would have kept at it indefinitely if the battery of my flashlight hadn't betrayed me. Then I transferred my attentions to the dormitory windows after lights out to trace my initials in the dust and grease exuded year after year by the pores of a thousand and more boys and girls breathing in the stultified air, because the windows were kept closed at the matron's instructions as fresh air would only have given us bad dreams anyhow, till I had covered the lower panes with scrawls and moved to the upper panes, balancing on the sill, not astounded by the change of seasons or the lighter hue entering the night sky or the fact that nothing can stop spring from coming every year.

Then it was summer and the exam came and went with the inevitable outcome.

'What's it all about?' That's the question I intended to put to the matron or the reverend or Brother Bartholemew, given the proper conditions, but the holidays arrived suddenly. Without warning, keys were turned in the locks of the classrooms, the windows were shuttered and with the others I was dispatched for what Brother Bartholemew, addressing the class on the last day of school, described as 'vocational training.'

Every day without intervention of solace we were marched from the school to the village: to the tannery where gutted horses hung upside down on hooks, or to the bleach works where head-scarved young girls sang heart-rending refrains with their arms up to the elbow in lye, while the foreman, a brute of a beast, pinched their bums in the steaming gloom to make them shriek with pretended fright and I pushed corks into bottles or hoisted dead horses into the air in one long day that stretched for eight weeks from July to August, approximate terms only and an artifice to arouse expectations of respite and eternal summer skies, the way poets say youth is supposed to be, when I never had any, rising in the morning to flop down late at night, my dreams so exhausted I didn't as much as glimpse them, for no wages, nothing, not a pittance. Every last penny was diverted to the matron and the reverend, sitting up in the study in the quiet of the long summer afternoons, listening to the radio or the light breeze that most likely ruffled the trees all summer long, drinking our blood.

With a bit more luck too, I would've later recalled nothing of that vast tract of vacation, those so-called holidays, if Kane hadn't disappeared, never to be heard of again.

Even that I could've got over, could've learned to accept, looking forward to another endless session of days all the way uphill to Christmas, over the precipice of the year to the next summer, when – who knows? – it might be my turn next, had Kane not started to come back in the heavy dreams I began to have, showing his insistent, frenetic face, his bland forehead sprinkled with glass beads, his mouth opening and closing like a fish. He was trying to tell me something, trying to say something I only made out eventually on that night when a sharp sound from the dormitory about me penetrated my dream. When I opened my eyes I knew it could only have come from over there beyond the dormitory, along the corridor and up the three wax-clothed steps to the landing; from the closed door of the study with its symmetry of panels where the sound must have been coming night after night after night since the day Kane vanished.

In the cold draught I listened at the door, then bent down to look through the keyhole into the bright room, brighter than day, almost feeling sorry for the two of them because even night made no difference to the intractable habit of their constant motion, condemned as they were never to lie down to rest but always to be moving as they were now, the reverend at the desk obscuring the matron opposite him, the matron watching what he was doing with her restless unblinking eyes, seated just as he was, upright, approving the rustling sound he made as he rummaged on the top of the desk.

Then I saw what it was on the desk. It was a big bulky parcel of newspapers he was unwrapping and from which he took something and sat down on the chair so I was able then to see the matron do the same, dip her hand into the parcel and take out something white and put it to her mouth. Because it was white I saw when the reverend waved the bone or whatever it was he was chewing on, in the direction of the portrait, and said something to the matron, who looked up with the silver fork in her hands, her jaws moving and a dark trickle running down both sides of her chin from the corners of her mouth, not caring to wipe it away.

Then the reverend took out a handkerchief and as he reached across the top of the desk he must have brushed the paper inadvertently, very lightly, because it made that sound newspaper always makes when disturbed, that sort of crinkling sound that's like nothing else.

And because I couldn't believe what I'd seen, I didn't close an eye during the night that followed but kept on the move, treading the dark corridors, sitting for respite in an empty classroom, going out into the yard to run my hand along the wall from one end to the other, through the gate into the vegetable garden at the rear of the school to shuffle through the blue leaves of the turnips and cabbages, heavy with dew, and listen for a moment to the snores of the pig slumped in his sty in the corner, until the early morning bell rang as if the day were beginning.

I couldn't keep that up for long and when the tension of not knowing became unbearable, I crept down to the study on the quiet of an afternoon and in the opened drawer of the desk, pulled at the wet soggy papers of the parcel, having to pick at it with my nails, pick the wet, ink-run paper from the softness underneath, saturated with the black ink, so that it was only when a piece of the flesh rose up with a torn strip of paper and the bright crimson-red spurted out in a fresh flow, thick as a tear-drop, that it came back to me what that familiar shape resembled, round like a ball, big as a football. Even then I didn't recognize the face, so ravaged it was, pecked at by vultures, and it was only after I closed the drawer I saw Kane's white face in front of me, suspended in the centre of the room, his mouth no longer opening and closing because I knew then what it was he'd been trying to tell me, what it was he kept coming back to mouth in my haunted dreams, that they'd killed him, poor innocent Kane; killed him and eaten him, a piece at a time out of a newspaper, those two monsters.

I grabbed the certificates from the bottom drawer, the only proof that any of us had ever existed, and bolted down to the dormitory, hiding them where I thought they'd never find them, under the mattress of Kane's vacated bed, planning to move them somewhere even safer, such as to the sand of the beach, as soon as I could.

But a few days later Brother Bartholemew threw up his hands and said there was no point going on. There's no point in continuing, he said. I would never learn, would never know a single thing and might just as well be making myself useful working with the janitor, shovelling the coal all the way through the week from one Monday to the next, down the shute and into the cellar and across the cellar and onto the big heap that slowly diminished as the coal went from there into the furnace, inevitably attracting the Monday that was coming as it burned, glowed, sending boiling water up the painted steel pipes into the room over-head to keep their study at a constantly over-heated temperature, all the year round.

I was quite happy there, drinking tea out of big mugs with the kindly old janitor at his little table in the little room at the back of the furnace, sleeping during the day on the striped mattress, listening occasionally to the sound of footsteps on the bare floorboards above my head during the night when the reverend and the matron became so restless and paced about and I wondered if it were true they could move unhindered through bolted doors, pass with ease through walls.

But I was left in peace on my own, and what seemed like years later, when the janitor didn't come back, I continued to shovel the coal that kept arriving on Monday or whatever day it had become by then, concentrating all my remaining strength on the cold food that came down on a plastic plate each day on the dumb waiter, with almost nothing else to think about except the nagging memory of those certificates hidden under Kane's mattress.

It wasn't just this that bothered me. I could've got over those certificates all right. It was the stillness that had started to sweep the school when I awoke during the afternoons, making the roaring of the furnace seem louder. Not the stillness in itself, but that lately it had become larger and wider with more space intervening between the shouts of someone at play in the yard above, footsteps on the concrete, or the bell ringing, until eventually the silence became so wide and so long it stretched from one end of the day to the other and the leaves, dead on the trees, as if winter had come forever, chinked like metal when the wind drove across the yard. It was as if the holidays had come at the wrong time of the year.

I couldn't help it. I couldn't stay down there any longer, especially since I couldn't remember the last time I'd heard a sound from the study above.

The night I entered the dormitory again after such a long absence, the door was ajar and the beds vacated. The bundle was still there where I'd hidden it. I seized it from under the mattress and just as I did so I heard the boards creak in the study. The sound magnified as it came down the long corridor in the pitch dark and in through the open door.

Fast as I could I raced with the bundle down the corridor out into the yard, across the playground and over the wall, ploughing through the fields of black grass and stopping when I could go no further, at the sea, on the sloping sand.

With no time to lose I scrabbled in a frenzy, digging deeper and deeper to make a hole to hide the parchments, and had just put them in and filled up the hole and was smoothing out the sand when out of the corner of my eye I saw her shoes just a few inches away and like pig's eyes the straps were fastened at one side with a tiny pink button with a black spot in the centre just to show how hard was the pink on the outside, and the flesh was bulging over the tight straps of the matron's shoes. Holding it in were two legs encased in silk stockings that could easily have been covered with dusted fish scales. The stockings were so filled with blood that it was difficult to bring into focus the legs that stopped at the hem of the heavy woollen material, heavy as lead, because the hem didn't move even though that part of the beach is notorious for the strong cold wind that can rise up suddenly and without warning, blowing people over and over. It hadn't started up yet, hadn't started to nudge the sand against the shoes, the sand that was so loose at the top and ready to stir, and when it did it would cover the gleaming black surface with fine dust and make the skirts of the matron tremble.

I looked up then, quite deliberately, when I'd finished what I was doing, feeling the heat hit the back of my neck from the sun that was rising behind me above the flat sea. As it rose it threw my shadow across the sand all the way to the dunes, at the same time as a few grains of sand careered skittering across the surface of the packed beach, impelled by the slightest of breezes.

'We've been looking for you,' the matron said. 'What have you done with them?'

I let some more sand filter through my closed fist and said, 'It's too late now.' I said I knew all about it. Knew what she and the reverend had been up to and that they couldn't do a thing about it. 'You won't catch me asleep,' I said.

And wasting no more time in talk she turned and started back up the beach again towards the reverend, outlined all the more sharply in his black garments by the morning sky – the towers and crenellated walls of the school just visible from where I knelt, over the other side of the dunes.

It wasn't quite the same down in the furnace after that. I kept at it a few more months, sweating over the coal, snatching cat-naps in the afternoons and even, by way of experiment, sleeping some nights too.

No one came. I started to go out into the yard during the

day, shuffling through the thick carpet of golden leaves that littered the ground, looking through the dirty broken window panes into the classrooms, recalling the rows and rows of heads and Brother Bartholemew smacking the ruler down on his desk as the pupils intoned to his beat.

Once or twice I ventured into the school itself. Text books and torn jotters littered the corridors, the classroom doors hung open on their hinges and through the cracked panels of the ceilings along the corridors, pigeons cooed in the rafters and let fall their droppings.

Everyone was gone. The school was abandoned. But it took me a few more weeks before I summoned the courage to do what I had to do, which was go back through the dusty dormitory, along the corridor and up the steps to the door of the study.

A scratched suitcase had been placed by the door and the door was ajar. The reverend and the matron were still there, in the same position they had been that first night when I looked through the keyhole, the position I would always recall them in, she seated, he poised over the bureau, their fingers like the claws of petrified birds placed on the crumpled newspaper on the desk. The paper didn't rustle above the barely audible sound of my tread across the carpet. When I was right behind the reverend I breathed on his grey wrinkled neck, so slowly I couldn't tell whether he was alive or dead. To make sure, I struck him on the side of the head such a blow with my fist it made a dull sound like an eggshell cracking and the fetid fluid spewed from his skull as he fell. Then I saw the drained, ancient face of the matron and what they had been pecking at – all that was left of the entire House of Charity – what looked like a shrivelled, petrified thumb or a finger, atrophied, all that remained of the corpses between a few old bones, gnawed of all flesh. Before she could even begin to raise her eyes, slumped in her ponderous weight, in the heavy clothes that held her down that day more than any other as if she had been drowned for years in the sea, I strangled her against the wall, crushing an old shinbone to her dust-dry throat expelling the last gasp of air she had taken in years ago and never let out.

Without waiting for the moment when my heart would start to beat again I dragged the two of them down the steps and into the cold-room in the kitchen and hung them on the meat hooks, their eyes wide open, as if being dead made no difference.

And then, as if for the first time in all the years I had passed in the House of Charity, it started to rain. Or as if in all the time I had been kept there it had been raining in a constant downpour and only now had it let up for me to notice the lull and the day coming through the clouds. I sat in the matron's seat, and pulling open all the drawers turned out their contents to discover the school notepaper and envelopes carrying the crest of the Ali Wong School for Errant Children. The phone began to ring and the voice said tradesmen were already on their way in vans up the long rutted avenues between the poplars, bringing supplies to stock the kitchen and the storerooms, bringing the news that by some miracle children speaking their own names, names I knew, had been found on the doorsteps of the village and were recognized by everyone. And then I started to remember myself again, as I really am, as I always will be now that I can't grow any bigger, in my favourite spot, under the sunflowers and the intertwining vines on the sunporch of the old House of Charity looking onto the garden, at four o'clock in the afternoon, waiting for the first day of the new term to arrive, in my tweed suit the colour of stewed turnips, waiting for the bus to come up from the village and load the children in and take them down to the beach, while upstairs the restorer is working on the oil painting, scraping off the faces of the Board of Governors with a razor blade and painting in the faces of the children and my face, so that no one will ever remember what the others looked like, so it'll seem they never walked this earth.

But you can't really expect everything to turn out the way you plan, because when the first day of the new term did arrive and the children from the village were seated round the long table in the dining hall waiting for the celebratory banquet to begin, I went downstairs to the kitchen to bring up the meat from the cold room and they were gone. Both of them, the reverend and the matron. All that was left was her blouse and her cardigan and her thick woollen skirts hanging from the hook, with her shoes dangling at the ends of her slack stockings like rag dolls', and beside them the reverend's black coat, black hat and black shoes, covered with hoar frost, stiff and equally empty.

I decided against slaughtering the pig. Instead, we ate bread and drank water at that banquet to which I'd also invited all the past pupils of the home, to tell them the news: that they hadn't been abandoned after all but had been stolen. I also recovered the proof from the beach to show them, in case they didn't believe what those two vampires were up to, selling children into slavery so they could take their place in the long row of black-coated figures staring out from the painting into the study from the centuries ever behind, so that nothing would ever change and everything would remain the way it was, the way it's always been in this place they call the world, repeating itself endlessly without remission or respite.

But even the banquet and the noise of the children playing outside in the yard or the sound they make going home each evening to the village isn't always enough to drown the memory of those two. In blurred photographs in newspapers, between snatches of song on the radio, I catch their movement as they wander tirelessly, restless, about the globe.

I can't be sure. I've imagined them, too, in a rickety train passing between cactus plants under a purple sky, rolling on the wooden seats going across parched plains and cracked mud-flats on their way to a meeting with an interested party contracted through an ad in the personal columns of *The Times*, to sell more children into slavery, be where the plague is raging hardest.

Because all the time they're changing form, are, for a moment, in a crowd waiting for a boat or a plane, are passing in a bus lit up at night on the highway, are going through customs lugging heavy suitcases, lurching in the corridors of fast trains. That's why I don't go about much anymore. Even during the day I hear the beat of vampire wings. I prefer to stay here at the window of the study, smelling the breeze that comes up from the sea, looking down onto the vegetable garden where the porker roots and snorts, his incisors flashing.

I'm glad now we didn't eat him or those other two either. I don't think it would have made any difference if we had. There was just no way of making sure they stayed dead. I know, I tried.

INCIDENT IN
LE LAVANDOU

Ronald Frame

The view was not as Miss Simm remembered it. The plane trees must have been the same ones – their tops were just visible – but white buildings pressed in on the old streets from all sides and she could see no plan to the town. There must be one – she might find it down at street level – but the longer she looked the more confused she felt she was becoming.

She finished dressing in front of the wardrobe mirror, with the open balcony doors and the blue Riviera sky behind her. She thought, perhaps if I'd lived here I should scarcely have been conscious of all the changes in half a century? She stood straightening her skirt, pulling at the cuffs of her blouse, telling herself how different it was from Largs. *I'm here, I managed the journey after all, there's life in the old girl yet.*

But when the wardrobe door and the mirror swung back on creaking hinges the view and the confidence disappeared, and she felt elderly and rather foolish and terribly Scottish in her tweeds as she looked about her to find the canvas shoes she'd brought with her as a concession to the town's hot streets.

Madame Lépront stood drinking her coffee at the little ornamental balcony, watching the patterns of life on the streets far beneath her. It had been her idea that the junk-filled attic of the villa could be turned into a commodious, sunny apartment, and the result justified all the hard graft of long ago: a quiet, forgotten spot high above people's

83

heads, easily kept in order, cool in summer when the shutters were closed and, with its low ceilings and because the rooms underneath were always occupied by tenants, not too expensive to heat in winter. Bright and airy, it suited widowhood. Few people suspected that anyone lived up here among the rafters, which even the pigeons had abandoned by the time they got down to the conversion work.

She took mouthfuls of the hot milky coffee. She swallowed it noisily, in gulps, and heard herself. Her manners had suffered a bit since Guy's death. When she'd married she'd had to get used to the French way of attacking food with such relish, and now nearly fifty years later she couldn't undo herself of the habit. She might have passed for 'Made in France'.

Madame Lépront always enjoyed the early heat of the day and she liked to feel it warming the stone of the balcony under her bare feet and the roof tiles she leaned her back against. Later on in the day she wasn't so comfortable with it. She stayed indoors, or she would make her forays in the car; if it happened she was meeting someone and she had no choice about being out, she kept as much as possible to the shade. About six o'clock the sun lost its spite and she reappeared on the balcony to have a drink, whatever there was on the sideboard. A couple of hours later the sun turned to the colour of a blood-orange as it sank slowly behind Africa. The sky would have a mysterious greenish tinge some nights; on others it would suddenly catch fire from the sun, flaming to crimson, and she would watch as other colours composed themselves around the red-hot core, vermilion, couleur de rose, then lighter fleshier pinks, cooling to topaz and Indian yellow and lemon on the extremities.

The heat, thought Miss Simm, the heat: that would have been the worst of it, I should never have adjusted.

But the skies, *they* would have been something to see, evening after evening. Maybe I would have taken up sketching, water-colours, pastels, gouache: maybe even proved myself quite adept.

Maybe.

Indoors again – the coffee doing its work and pepping her up after her night's deep sleep – Madame Lépront dressed. Summer-wear was straightforward: a pale cotton shift and espadrilles, it couldn't have been easier. She combed her hair back over her ears, and applied a very little, very discreet liner to her eyelids.

She looked hard at herself. Her face had become thinner with the years, and longer if that was possible: or perhaps it was because she only saw French faces that she viewed her own differently now. Decades of sun had bleached her hair, so that she was scarcely able to recognize the dark-fringed young woman in photographs, posed with her mother and father and her sister and two brothers. The sun had also toughened her skin and lined it, and sometimes she smiled rather sadly when she told people about her foreign youth and her 'peaches-and-cream' complexion, as the term used to be.

This morning, though – thinking positively – she felt that her appearance had an *authenticity* about it which it never used to have. She was wholly herself, she didn't need to satisfy other people's expectations of how she should look. The longer she lived, the simpler the presentation and final version of herself became. For that she thanked her years in France, now – unbelievably – two-thirds of her life.

'*Une tasse de thé, s'il vous plaît. Comment? Un thé? Très bien. Pour moi seule. Thé de chine. Merci.*'

Miss Simm had never felt comfortable with such an extrovert language. Passing the simplest remark involved contorting your face to pronounce some absurd, indecently sensuous-sounding hotch-potch of syllables.

At least the waiter nodded his head; but curtly, Miss Simm thought. Frumpy British types obviously weren't worth humouring. No tip for *you*, she decided, and the little revenge in prospect reassured her.

Miss Simm placed her day-old *Telegraph* on top of the table, and she laid her room key on top of it. What would her friends be doing at home, she wondered. Probably wondering what *she* was doing with herself and why on earth should she want to hire herself off to the South of France at *her* age. They'd be puzzling about that, and about the other matters that preoccupied them, which filled their days and hers because there was no getting away from them: annuities, the sloth and miserliness of the faceless dispensers of company pensions, the tardiness of lawyers dealing with a cousin's will, a shares statement, the red print demand on an electricity bill which had already been paid, the new rates estimate, an accountant's fee for 'offices' rendered, the state of the roses in the landscaped gardens of the block where they lived.

How odd that she was suddenly feeling so disengaged about it. But, she thought, maybe in another couple of days' time I shall have reverted again?

Normally she didn't go on holiday alone, she went with one of her neighbours, or with someone she'd worked with in the company her brother used to manage and which he had 'invited' her to lend her services to – and the conversation wherever their travels took them would inevitably return to home, and to the past. This time the past that concerned her was known only to herself and to her twin cousins in Strathpeffer, the three of them being the sole survivors of that family group who'd come south in 1936. And perhaps – just perhaps – it was still known to *him*: the Frenchman she'd never been able to forget even though she couldn't have described his face to save her life and whose own life had been more or less a mystery to her, then and ever since.

Madame Lépront enjoyed her privacy and independence. No one here saw her comings and goings, even though the rest of the building was occupied. The villa was hers now – it had come to Guy through the will of an aunt – and perhaps she was allowed her privacy out of respect, she couldn't be sure. 'La Châtelaine' and all that.

She drew an income from the tenants, here and in several other properties Guy had bought. Nowadays she was a bona fide businesswoman: at this comparatively late juncture in her life she had the self-assurance and the financial say-so – and, still, the mental and physical stamina – to be able to badger lawyers and accountants, and she made it a point of honour not to be brow-beaten or fobbed off by any of them. She could be quite charming when she chose to be, but that never obscured the fact that her husband's death had turned her into a very determined and very knowing woman where the practicalities of business were concerned. People could tell by the authority of her body walking into a room, the set of her face, the shine in her eyes. She'd had to work at it, but now she wouldn't have wanted to be any other way than she was.

She closed her front door behind her, heard the lock turn, then she hurried down the three flights of stairs with a swiftness of foot that she knew belied her years.

Well, at seventy-two one presumes there just isn't the energy – the vim – left, thought Miss Simm. Not for gallivanting off to foreign parts. Even if this isn't exactly gallivanting, not quite. And of course these aren't just *any* run-of-the-mill foreign parts . . . She crumpled the paper napkin and, after hesitating, let it drop on to her plate of croissant crumbs.

She couldn't have taken to French breakfasts, she was

quite positive about that. Too much fuss for nothing. And why did croissants always *have* to have that greasy feel to them? Better off with her Bran Buds, and one slice of wholemeal toast, and the Frank Cooper's, and Algie's no-nonsense Ceylon tea.

'Better off as I am.' The words were on the tip of her tongue to say, but she realized there was no one to hear if she were to open her mouth and say them, and she also wondered if she was really the person best qualified to judge.

The words lacked, somehow, *conviction*.

No one in Le Lavandou was certain how old Madame Lépront was, but it was general knowledge that she'd first come to the town in the 1930s, when she was someone else, the younger daughter of a foreigner and his wife on holiday here – a businessman, a 'whisky broker' hadn't she said, a most bizarre occupation – when she had been a pale and fragile young woman, shy beneath her fringe of dark hair.

The most precise of her neighbours guessed that now she must be seventy or thereabouts: 'guessed', Madame Lépront was perfectly aware. (In warmer climes, she knew, it's often easier to make a riddle of numerals – sixty-five, seventy, seventy-five – among faces prematurely wrinkled and veined and stoically smiling under their uniform tans. In sunshine you can dress to virtually any age you choose: other people are more charitable about any sartorial mis-calculations and errors of taste, it's merely amusing – for a brief time – then assimilated into the everyday way of things. Madame Lépront realized that public opinion was decided that on the whole she dressed with sense but also with some 'chic', in styles that would have looked just as well worn by a woman half her age. It was a verdict that gave her much secret satisfaction.)

Guy Lépront's widow stood in the downstairs hallway opening her morning's mail. Sunlight flooded through the open double-doors and washed over the checkerboard of black and white tiles. Vaguely, as she read, she was conscious of the heady brew of the garden's perfumes: pine, floribunda roses, rosemary, orange blossom, the inevitable lavender that the town was named after. The fragrance and the heat lapping round her always made her feel well-disposed, even when her correspondence was about financial business and she was required to make some brisk mental calculations there and then. The men she dealt with in the business line were there for a purpose, they had specific duties which she was paying them to perform and she refused to be intimidated or confused by their manner: when they wrote to her they were required to express themselves, please, with particular clarity. '*Elucidez, s'il vous plaît. Avec concision.*'

Madame Lépront bundled the assortment of letters and postcards into her bag, shut the clasp, and dropped the bag into her basket. Walking down the front steps and across the gravel, out of the villa's shadow, she felt buoyant and prepared for whatever the day might be bringing her.

Back upstairs in her bedroom, Miss Simm debated whether or not she should take her plastic mackintosh and rainmate with her. Yes, she decided, yes, I *shall* take them.

It always paid to be on the safe side. Better safe than sorry. And who knew more about the safe and sensible and least hazardous way of living this life than herself?

On cloudless mornings when she felt like walking on the balls of her feet, Madame Lépront could believe she'd taken full and proper advantage of all the opportunities that had come her way in this life. She'd allowed life to take her, not always where she'd been expecting to go, but where it seemed to have determined that she should be taken. Life's plans for her hadn't been the same as her family's, and she'd had to persist in the face of their opposition. She could have heeded the puritan designs of her father and mother and the clamouring maiden aunts and made of herself whatever they would have decided according to the models of their class and country: a stainless wife-to-be for a redoubtable fiancé, or a meek and modest stay-at-home daughter, or – had they been willing to allow her a little more independence, plus an allowance – she might have become an untested, prim-mouthed young woman settling prematurely into spinsterhood in a decent community of like souls.

Instead she lived on the Côte d'Azur and in sunshine: and if there must be shadows, they were no threat to her, not now after fifty years. When her children and grandchildren quizzed her gently about her past, she let them see that it was neither here nor there to her – concealing nothing that they wanted to know – but that really she preferred to think of the life she had shared with *them* as her true history. She had given much thought to the past, however, in a more abstract sense. She'd often wondered if people's lives don't all contain some emotional apogee, some heightened and climactic omega of experience, its highwater mark, which might occur at any point – early or late – and turns into an epiphany, a moment of revelation. One of two consequences ensues from the event: either everything else that follows proves a falling-off and tailing-away and nothing is ever felt so intensely again – or the opposite happens, the incident becomes a pointer to possibilities that previously hadn't occurred to you and you turn towards them, freshly confident and cast in a new frame of mind.

Confident, but with the uncomfortable consciousness of betrayal. For hadn't she committed the one heinous and finally unpardonable crime: she'd left the country where she'd grown up and its northern climes, she'd abandoned its morality and the bracing winds and grey days of soft Atlantic drizzle for marriage and the white Mediterranean light and empty Latin noons and green African twilights of this lavender town, Le Lavandou?

* * *

After breakfast Miss Simm stood in the hallway of the hotel consulting a map on the wall. Unconcerned voices passed up and down the corridor behind her as she cocked her head this way and that to get a better perspective on things.

She tried to spot where it had happened. With her index finger she jabbed at various points on the map, intersections where streets crossed. Perhaps she would recognize the place when she came upon it.

In those days, ironically, there had been so much less motor-driven traffic to have to be careful about. What had got into her she had never been able to understand. Was it like vertigo, which (she'd read somewhere) is supposed to mask an unconscious wish to step off a high point and experience the elation and oblivion of plunging downward: or, like insomnia, which (she'd read somewhere else) is really the fear of falling asleep and discovering what thoroughly nasty and sordid imaginings you might conjure up in your dreams.

She'd walked off the edge of the pavement on to the road and in front of the car because . . . Because . . . Not because she'd guessed the man, *that* man, would reach out his arm and grab her and haul her back: she only knew him as a face – a handsome face – from the hotel, and it was only by chance that she'd turned and looked behind her a few seconds before the incident occurred and seen that he was there. Maybe it was because she'd disorientated herself slightly, turning her head on her shoulders to look round, that the episode had happened? Or could there have been deeper causes why she'd stepped on to the road at the very instant the car was rounding the corner? – the memory of Alistair Forbes waiting at home, in douce grey Glasgow, and the prospect of, first, the inevitable return to Scotland after their visit to Aunt Bessy in Menton and, then, the decision she would have to make before she saw Alistair Forbes and his mother again. Perhaps her backward glance at the man – someone she'd noticed no more than half-a-dozen times and whom she knew nothing about – had disturbed her morning peace, it had prompted the thought of Alistair Forbes (never very far from her mind, but less insistent when she was walking in sunshine): and the incident that followed had been set in motion by her subconscious acting?

Or the quality of the light, could it have been? Had the sun been in her eyes on the crossing, and that was why she hadn't been able to see the car's hushed approach?

She'd been dazed for several seconds afterwards. Faces swam in front of hers, buildings teetered, the trees jigged. Then she'd focused, and it was the man she'd found she was looking at.

How solicitous he'd proved himself, how concerned everyone else – her family and their friends – had been for her. Concerned and also, she'd guessed, anxious and uneasy to know how it could have happened: as if suspecting that so terrible a thing couldn't have happened merely by chance, because how perilous then must every action in our lives become?

Madame Lépront ran her eyes down her shopping list. One person required almost as much as two, that was the strange thing. Two people *could* live as cheaply as one, not that economy had ever been a consideration with them both.

Buying for one sometimes seemed a futile occupation. But she had her family to owe an obligation to, and she was Guy's widow, with all its responsibilities to his memory. There had been so much – there was still so much – which she should feel grateful to her late husband for having given her: even this very air to breathe.

Without the incident happening, Miss Simm knew – the car turning the corner – the man wouldn't have had the excuse to see her as he was given permission to do afterwards. Otherwise her mother wouldn't have welcomed him to their table in the hotel dining-room of an evening, she wouldn't have allowed him to show them the lie of the coast and the rocky inland terrain as he did on half a dozen picnic expeditions. Frenchmen had always been untrustworthy on principle, but *he* was unconditionally exonerated of the faults of his race and granted a free pardon. If he hadn't had such excellent reflexes that he'd been able to shoot out his arm and tip her out of the car's path that day, she would most certainly not have found herself dining alone with a gallant foreign gentleman on a restaurant terrace strung with vines above a wild sea crashing on to boulders. In all probability she would have been dead.

By the time she was meeting him alone, unchaperoned, her life seemed to have gone off at an improbable tangent, she was suddenly walking on an unlikely track, further and further from the landmarks she recognized. At twenty-two years old she wasn't quite prepared for it, nor for her second offer of marriage in a troubled season. In another year's time – who was to say? – perhaps she might have been.

Perhaps the car had turned the corner a year too soon?

Madame Lépront glided silkily through the network of lanes that webbed the town. She felt cool in her washed-pink cotton shift. It billowed out behind her, in the fashionable style. She had good enough legs still to be able to go about with them bare. The espadrilles couldn't have been a better fit for her feet, and they might – in her current mid-morning frame of mind – have had wings.

Through her dark lenses she was aware that people were looking at her. She hoped they weren't playing the guessing-game about age: not that she was ashamed, but you *are* – the hoariest cliché in the book – as old or as young as you feel. Sometimes she felt rather less in command of herself, when the weather changed and the salt wind blowing inland over the rooftops seeped through the rubber seals on the windows and made twinges in her arms and shoulders and back. But that was only occasionally, and no one escapes scot free.

A few people were in the habit of exchanging 'good day' with her and she would drop a reply over her shoulder. She now passed as a native – and anyone would have been hard put to conclude that she was not. The language hadn't come easily to her, not until her first child was born, and then all the bits and pieces had seemed to fit into place. '*Ecossaise*' she would reply if anyone did ever ask her where she was from originally, that rather than '*Anglaise*': it left people much less certain about what to expect of her, and she preferred that her past should belong somewhere on the misty perimeter edge of their imagination. She chose to believe that every departure and new beginning in life is like a skin being shed: a character is compounding itself, and while the past is inevitably a part of it, it shouldn't be allowed to make falsely demanding claims. It doesn't – or shouldn't – ever *own* anyone.

Miss Simm thought she had found the spot: then she wasn't so sure.

She couldn't quite get her directions. The names of the streets on the signposts meant nothing to her. Payot, Péri, Cazin. After fifty years the country had a different set of heroes and liberators to commemorate. Avenue des Martyrs-de-la-Résistance, avenue du Général de Gaulle, boulevard Winston Churchill, avenue des Commandos d'Afrique. She asked herself if they *could* possibly be the same plane trees in the square, if they weren't too sprightly to be the ones she'd walked under in 1936.

In those days the coast had also been a working one, and among the sights had been the schools of fishing boats chugging for the jetties after a day or night at sea. There were far fewer of the smacks now, only a handful. Of course there had been a 'plage' then too, and flashy cars with running boards and white tyres, family groups like her own eating from picnic hampers, but the two ways of life – the indigenous and the elegantly fanciful – seemed to coexist in her mind. Now most of the town's business had to do with the wholesale pursuit of pleasure – and frankly she was disappointed. Shops were like stalls, their wares spilling on to the pavement so that it took all her concentration to keep herself from being directed by the pressure of bodies towards the kerb. People ate and drank as they walked about, just as they did at home. One or two of the cafés, with their customers fenced in from the drifting crowds, had something of the charm and style of those in Aix or Avignon. She could remember a restaurant along the coast – remember it just, the details – with a trellis or pergola and a vine overhead, and candles under glasses on the tables, and a trio walking between the tables playing she'd forgotten what on their violins, and a man talking to her: the words turning to ether as soon as he spoke them, his face only a couple of feet from hers but crossed with those shifting blue shadows.

The past didn't *own* her, Madame Lépront knew. Nor was it an anchor. But her mind would play with it, turning it over as she turned over the curious debris of shells and sea life she found washed up by the tide on her beachcombing walks.

Thinking how, if she hadn't had an opportunity to meet Guy in the way she had, none of the rest would have happened. But how she might have had an opportunity to meet him at another time and place – and so the rest would still have happened, wouldn't it?

She was an optimist in these matters. If something is meant to occur, you may be given more than one chance, if you bungle the first. But it's up to you not to let it go a second time: fate has limited reserves of patience and doesn't tolerate fools, those who won't learn.

'My Robert the Bruce principle', she sometimes joked to those who would understand the parable of the spider and the watching king. Without it the Scots wouldn't have been the enterprizing, persevering race she knew they were, and which she had proved by her own example.

Conveniently, Miss Simm thought, I have presumed he must be dead – but what if he isn't?

She calculated. How old would he have been then, in 1936? Twenty-five or twenty-six, at least. Thirty at the outside. Add fifty to that.

It was perfectly possible that he *was* living: he was alive and well, walking along a promenade somewhere in white summer clothes, tanned and spry?

A bachelor? She'd stopped allowing for that possibility long ago, about the time she decided to call off her engagement to Alistair Forbes and watched Elspeth Colquhoun take her place. She had realized from people's shocked reactions in the two cities, Glasgow and Edinburgh (and also in such respectable havens as genteel Helensburgh and decorous Kilmacolm), that it was only the few hard-bitten cases who resisted the mating call, and that she'd chosen to do something quite unnatural.

He wouldn't have given up so easily, her Frenchman. On another evening in the same restaurant above the sea, the same scene would have repeated itself. She had imagined it so often. The girl who sits at the table listens to him and considers well as the trio coax such sweet music from their violins. The vine trellis maps an exactly similar grid of shadows, and this time the scene plays to its intended conclusion. The man smiles, so does the girl. His face and hands reach forward out of the blue shadows. The sea tumbles on the rocks far beneath them, its roar muted to polite, whispered sibilants. His companion smells lavender, a fragrance carried off the hills on the warm breath of the wind, and she dares to hope that all her life with the man will echo the happiness of these perfect moments.

Madame Lépront walked downhill with long, confident strides. She wore dark glasses against the sun's glare.

The town spread beneath her, and beyond were the wooded slopes of Cap Bénat. She glanced at the promenade and the leafy square: gardeners were laying the dust, and the cafés had set out their wicker chairs and tables to lure customers.

The narrow back streets were the quickest way down and she was familiar with all the short cuts. Even after all her years in other cities she knew her way about like a local-born. Curiously, though, something about the place eluded her – a spirit – which she imagined she might have felt if she'd been living in, say, Antibes or St-Jean-de-Luz. Maybe she hadn't been here long enough since her return to discover that sense of place, or was the town not quite big enough or old enough? The 'spirit' had escaped her fifty years ago when she'd first arrived, when her eyes had been blinded by the sea light and she'd lived in a dizzy muddle: morning excursions in the car to what was judged worth seeing, evenings at the hotel enduring unending meals, lazy beach afternoons under sun umbrellas, expeditions across the sand-strewn streets to dark, cool shops and a café with a yellow awning that served green drinks and where a grinning man played an accordion accompaniment while a woman in a long nasturtium-coloured dress like a kimono sang slow, dirge-like songs that never seemed to have a melody.

Now there were so many cafés and none of them had a yellow awning. Miss Simm searched but couldn't find it. Pop music seeped out of passing cars and floated down from upstairs rooms and wafted up from basements and she couldn't hear those tuneless songs any more that she used to listen to. The woman who sang them had had a painted face and most of the songs had been to do with Montparnasse and Saint-Germain. She used to wonder, why doesn't she go back to Paris if she's so homesick and spare us all? But the songs, their words and melodies forgotten now, had been woven into the woof of those oddly static, becalmed afternoons when she'd sat with her sister or brothers or cousins, sipping tea, watching the few cars pass, seeming – it occurred to her now – to be only waiting for something to happen to her.

They'd lived in half-a-dozen places, and she'd come back to Le Lavandou. She wasn't sure why. It wasn't what it had been. Along the coast road there were still quieter spots, coves hidden by rocks and pines, and a couple of superior restaurants she sometimes went to, with terraces above the sea. Friends wrote or rang or visited from Paris and Geneva, and there was no risk of losing touch. (From longer ago there were still two cousins alive, ensconced in a Scottish spa town, but that was as much as she knew about them.) Children and grandchildren existed on the fringes of that mental map which composed her knowable world, in Switzerland and Belgium and America, and she believed herself distantly indispensable to them and never an intruder on privacy or a burden to conscience. At the centre of so much attention, she lived contentedly alone.

Maybe she'd meant coming back to Le Lavandou to be a drawing-in of all the threads? Here it had begun for her, one summer before the War, when she was another person: a silly accident-that-almost-was, stepping on to the road without looking first for traffic, and a hand – *his* hand, Guy's hand – reaching out for her. Now she was only paying her own homage of sorts to that fleeting incident which had made her busy, practical, necessary life possible in the first place.

*　　*　　*

Miss Simm wondered why she wasn't getting the 'feel' of the streets. She had imagined that, somehow, instinct would guide her.

She was aware that people were looking at her, smiling in her face, but not for simple civility's sake. She felt her tweeds were hanging heavily from her; the inside of her waist band was sodden with perspiration; her canvas shoes pinched.

She walked along the pavement however she could, jostled by arms and shoulders and hips. In *her* day there had been nothing like this: the people who'd come then, the cognoscenti, had behaved with tact.

The proximity of so much unclothed flesh was alarming her. She smelt the sun oil: a rich chemical odour that seemed to be filling her head, weighing it like a stone.

Suddenly she thought she couldn't trust her knees to hold her up any longer. She looked anxiously to either side of her before reaching out for the trunk of a plane tree to steady herself.

Her head was spinning. She blinked her eyes several times. With the tips of her fingers she stroked the silvery smooth bark. That at least was real, and confirmable, whether it was a tree from *then* – that long ago – or later.

It worried her that 'then' could vanish with so little trace left behind: or, just as bad, that it could play these confusing tricks of identity, hiding up side streets where it knew she had no hope of finding it, changing its name and purpose and disguising itself behind smart, modern frontages and the swarms of smart, modern people.

Mystified, Miss Simm shook her head. Then, gingerly, she let go her fastness, the plane tree's trunk.

Screwing up her courage, she rejoined the tide of holiday-makers, and allowed herself to be carried along on the drift.

They moved more quickly than she or any of her friends were used to moving. Somehow, at a certain point in your life, you felt you should be spared the urgency to reach anywhere: what was coming to you would come, and whether you rushed there or not didn't make an iota of difference. But who would have understood that here, even if she'd been able to speak in their language?

The pavement burned through her shoes' thin soles. Her legs seemed to have hardly any strength left in them. If she'd heaped pebbles into her pockets – like Virginia Woolf in the biography from the library she'd once read – she couldn't have felt any more lethargic or doomed.

She stopped looking to her left or her right and gazed, blinkered, over the heads of those in front of her. She was still being stared at, she knew, by incredulous people trying to guess what had brought her here. Her Scottishness must be written all over her, her age must be a joke.

Madame Lépront was remembering something else for her shopping list.

What was important was always to have an active mind. You couldn't keep age at bay, so why not accept it in a spirit of good grace, with a modicum of enthusiasm even? She'd known people who'd been middle-aged in their twenties, and people in their forties who'd seemed older than their parents.

It was all a matter of the mind's willingness, she was quite certain: a successful life answered to a positive, assertive attitude.

Attitude. Acknowledging the unlikeliness of failure was the best means of ensuring that failure was avoided.

Madame Lépront kept the spectres where they belonged, in the shadows. Far from Helensburgh and Kilmacolm, a thousand miles away, she walked in sunshine, in the widening, brightening glare of day.

On the place Reyer Miss Simm was thinking of Largs.

At home in the block of flats most of her neighbours were contemporaries: slow, creaking, stooped in their varying

degrees. She and her friends took their daily constitu-
tionals on the sea front where the wind blew briskly; they'd
sold their real homes, their families had scattered far and
wide, and what they had left was Largs, and each other,
and the view across Gogo Water to Cumbrae and Bute
and the peak of Goat Fell, and that other, much more
intriguing prospect – the past.

As they walked to the Pencil at Bower Craig or to Barr-
fields or along the residential avenues, her group would
watch with impatience their less able acquaintances shuffling and halting; one woman was always speeded past them
in a wheel chair, as absurdly bright-cheeked as a baby in a
pram.

They must be here in Le Lavandou too, Miss Simm
thought, deposited in blocks of flats like filing cabinets –
human retrieval systems – but discreetly removed from
the biz, in some other part of the town.

As she walked on, willing one foot in front of the other,
she felt she had escaped from elsewhere – that she was
treading where she shouldn't, out of bounds now, that the
middle-aged in their holiday undress were looking at her
with the unkindest stares of all, as if she was a bearer of
bad news.

Ridiculous, she told herself, I'm hallucinating: it's the
heat's doing, and because I've found out there's nothing
whatsoever to discover. I should never have left Largs. I'm
a stay-at-home, I always was, Le Lavandou can't tell me
anything I don't know already. That all was really for the
best: that I decided according to the person I was, the one
heredity made of me, because I was born to certain parents
in a certain place far to the north of here at a certain point
in the history of human affairs when a properly-reared
young Scotswoman did not – most emphatically did *not* –
lose her heart to an olive-skinned, dark-eyed Frenchman,
however impeccably upright and principled and chivalrous
she afterwards discovered his reputation to be.

*   *   *

They'd lived well, she and Guy, to the full. The days had never been long enough for them, no sooner here than they were done. Like paper days being stripped off a calendar in films she'd seen. Their years together had flitted past, the allotted thirty-nine had been used up and she was left confused afterwards, unsure how she could have lived through so long a span and been so little conscious of its passing.

They'd balanced each other, she'd always felt. (Or did she mean 'complemented'?) Guy had been resolute, unpersuadable once he was decided on something; but also fair, willing to understand a weakness in another and why it occurred; he'd had a tender and romantic side to his nature, too, being so absurdly protective of her. Since Guy's death, she'd assumed those qualities to herself: the romantic impulse least successfully of all perhaps, because she'd been born a Scot but the kind who turns with age, not maudlin, but eminently practical and matter-of-fact.

Married to Guy, she'd felt she was one half of a whole: now she felt she was more than herself, she was one-and-a-half people, herself plus as much of Guy as she had managed to save.

He was with her, because so long as one of them was left, the other must be too, since they had been so close. She had no dealings with the widows – the handless kind or the guilty ones – who depended on their faith in mediums. A marriage was between two persons, and if mutual trust and confidence weren't there as a bond in the beginning they most definitely couldn't be learned in the hereafter.

It was the tramping and slithering of feet Miss Simm heard on all sides of her, then – further off, so she imagined, but really only yards away and separating her from the palms and the promenade wall – the groaning and screeching of traffic, engines straining, brakes squealing, horns blaring. There was a smell of burning rubber, and she wondered how the trees survived so bravely and shiny-leaved after years in the suffocating, choking atmosphere of fumes.

She looked forward, over the heads in front of her, blinkered against the watching faces to left and right of her. She could ask, try to ask, but she didn't know what exactly it was she was looking to find. It was her feelings she was relying on to tell her, her instincts. Relying on, but she couldn't be sure . . .

Then, just seconds later, it seemed she had no doubts at all. She suddenly stopped in her tracks. She'd reached the end of the block. Turning her back to the shore and the sea, she looked up at the front of the building nearest her and saw with a start the word 'Hotel' in old-fashioned script, shining through the paintwork from another era.

People jostled around her, oiled limbs passed brazenly by, and she continued to look up. What had its name been? The Hotel What?

She closed her eyes, trying to remember, trying to call it up, abracadabra it out of the past. A girl's name, wasn't it?

She opened her eyes slowly. She realized she was swaying on her feet. An arm reached out to steady her. Someone said something, in anxious-sounding French. She couldn't reply, not in kind, and she smiled as best she could.

'I think – I can manage, thank you,' she said in a croaky voice, meaning to sound game, plucky.

She turned round. Ahead of her the building on the other side of the street was modern, it had too much glass. Or – her eyes widened – perhaps the glazed terraces on the ground and first floors were only recent additions, to what was much older?

She tilted her head further back to take in the rest of the building. One second it seemed as close as could be, the next it was as distant as what had happened years ago, or had not happened.

She tried to focus, to concentrate, but her eyelids

wouldn't stay open. Her legs continued walking, but without any instruction from her that they should, no command at all. It was as if her limbs were another person's, or it was as if she was living in a stranger's body, she had been for years and only now did the ruse declare itself, at the very last moment.

Her legs carried her forward and there was no stopping them, nothing she could do even if she'd had the will. The traffic pulled and sucked like the tides, the people on all sides of her fixed her on her course, the pavement was like a channel running under her.

But just ahead the pavement shelved and as she felt her legs start to give way beneath her she waited in that split second for a saving hand to reach out and grab her.

It didn't come.

Instead one side of her seemed to be blasted away with the impact, her right hand scorched on the metal.

Someone screamed. She heard, somewhere on the periphery of the moment, shouts.

Then she had the illusion of flying as Le Lavandou bore on her from every angle.

She was inside a kaleidoscope, she found, she was rattling round and round with the pieces, far from the sounds. Topsy-turvy, head-over-heels, round and round and round and round . . .

In another part of the town Madame Lépront continued on her way, sublimely unaware of any mishap anywhere else.

Her shift blew behind her, her feet hardly touched the cobbles or paving stones in their haste to reach wherever it was they were taking her. She felt – even for her – unusually light and weightless.

She listened to the muffled roar of traffic beneath her in the crowded streets: revving cars, spluttering motorcycles, air brakes sighing on lorries, the tourist coaches sitting with their engines rumbling to keep the air-conditioning turning over.

Le Lavandou wasn't what it had been, but nowhere was: and it wasn't as it would be in another fifty years, nothing like.

She slowed as she walked downhill, towards the sea that gave the town its raison d'être. She removed her dark glasses and dropped them into her basket. Her eyes filled with bright crystalline light: it poured inside her head.

A breeze blowing uphill ruffled the folds of her fashionably pale pink shift around her knees.

A siren separated itself from the traffic noises and the squawking of seabirds overhead. She noticed an ambulance passing at the bottom of the street, with blue beacons flashing.

Momentarily her brow furrowed, but only for a moment – then the skin became smooth again and her expression cleared.

She carried on walking. Her shift blew out behind her. To anyone who might have seen, the breeze would have seemed to cut clean through her, just like a spirit.

Feather-light, as light as air, she passed on, unhurried and uncomplicated, like someone with only the livelong day to fill and not a thought in her head to hold her back.

Then finally – in blissful, relieved slow motion and beyond pain – Miss Simm was diving
                              diving
                              diving
In her mind's eye she caught a last backwards glimpse of herself, reduced to just a speck, a particle.

Deeper and deeper, she was fathoms down in the silence, diving for the vanishing point, disappearing into the cool blue wastes of all that annihilating summer sky.

HENRY AND JOYCE
AND THE 33-YEAR-OLD WOMAN

Alex. Hamilton

Henry was a great friend of mine and Joyce was a great friend of Henry's. Joyce was a great friend of mine and Henry was a great friend of Joyce's. I haven't seen Joyce for, maybe, eleven years but Henry and I meet from time to time. Perhaps every six months on average.

There was a time when I would have dismissed any such projected absences as not merely impossible but quite inconceivable. Henry and I were close, close and Joyce and I were closer, in some ways, than Henry and I ever could be. Joyce and Henry were close too, in some ways closer than ever I was with either of them. And yet, in some ways, Henry and I were closer than ever I was with Joyce or Joyce was with Henry or Henry was with Joyce or Joyce was with me.

I don't know where Joyce is and nor does Henry. Perhaps she'll read this and reestablish contact. That would be good.

Three or four or a hundred years ago, Henry was living and working in Edinburgh and, from second- or third-hand reports, Joyce too had been sighted there.

Deploring their habits, feeling their ages and trying to prolong their youths, Henry and three colleagues took up the game of squash. Foolish, perhaps, but they are all still alive and, wiser, have given it up now.

One day, as Henry and his opponent approached their court, they passed the two people of whom they were relieving it. One was a 33-year-old woman.

'Hello.'

Henry's face brightened in unprompted joy as he recognized her.

'How are you?' said Henry.

'I'm fine, thank you,' said the 33-year-old woman. 'How are *you*?'

'Oh, fine,' said Henry. 'Fine. What are you doing? Do you stay here? Are you working? It's so good to see you again.'

'Again?' said the 33-year-old woman. 'I'm sorry. I've never seen you before in my life.'

'But it's me,' said Henry. 'Henry. You must remember me, Joyce?'

'Henry?' said the 33-year-old woman. 'Joyce? I'm sorry. I don't know anybody called Henry – and my name isn't Joyce.'

She didn't say what her name was but at least she was smiling. So, although Henry felt foolish, he didn't feel accused.

'Oh,' said Henry, 'I'm sorry. I thought you were somebody else. An old friend of mine. Her name's . . .'

'. . . Joyce,' said the 33-year-old woman.

Henry smiled and nodded, she smiled back, Henry said sorry, she said that was all right, they smiled again and Henry went onto the court and squashed the life out of his opponent by way of taking revenge on himself.

Three or four or a hundred weeks later, as Henry and his workmate approached their court, they passed the two people of whom they were relieving it. One was a 33-year-old woman.

'Hello.'

Henry's face brightened in unprompted joy as he recognized her.

'How are you?' said Henry.

'I'm fine, thank you,' said the 33-year-old woman. 'How are *you*?'

'Oh, fine,' said Henry. 'Fine. What are you doing? Do you stay here, Are you working, It's so good to see you again.'

'It's good to see you, too, Henry,' said the 33-year-old woman. 'I'm really flattered that you remember me.'

'Flattered?' said Henry. 'Don't be silly. How could I ever forget you, Joyce?'

'Ah,' said the 33-year-old woman, 'so you have, then.'

'Pardon?' said Henry. '*Have* what?'

'Forgotten me,' said the 33-year-old woman.

'But,' said Henry, 'how can I have forgotten you? I remembered you, I stopped you and I'm talking to you, Joyce.'

'Ah,' said the 33-year-old woman, 'you haven't remembered me, you haven't stopped me and you're not talking to me at all.'

'What?' said Henry.

'I'm a 33-year-old woman,' said the 33-year-old woman. 'Three or four or a hundred weeks ago you stopped me at this court, were delighted to see me, enquired after my welfare and were dismayed when I didn't recognize you. That's when you introduced yourself as Henry, Henry, and that's why I remember you. In fact, it's not likely that I'll ever forget you. Now. Bye.'

The 33-year-old woman smiled and walked away.

'Bye,' said Henry, and gave up squash.

It really didn't agree with him.

THE BEAUTIFUL PEOPLE
OF JUAN LES PINS

Iain MacDonald

The student awoke at about seven o'clock to find himself
in the company of ten or twelve winos, blinking in the sunshine and swearing with more or less good nature at a
gendarme. They had not been there when he was directed
to the place in the early hours of the morning, he was sure
of that. One of them he had seen the day before as he left
the station, sitting at a corner with a sign saying '*J'ai faim –
merci.*' The cop whistled as he wandered round the untidy
little group, prodding a reluctant body with his foot, picking up an empty bottle and dropping it in a nearby bin.

'*Bonjour, bonjour !*'

'*Bonjour,*' replied the student, though nobody else did.
He rolled up his sleeping bag and packed it in his rucksack.
He didn't wish to appear to be in a hurry, but he didn't
stop to shake out the sand or to greet his companions. His
money and cheques were safe in his borrowed money-belt –
there was no need to check those. He allowed himself one
last steady look at the strangely picturesque group of
hippies, the scattered wine bottles, the immaculate gendarme hovering with an almost motherly expression on his
face. One last look to imprint it on his memory, that he
might faithfully recall the scene for flatmates, mother, girl-
friend. He shouldered his rucksack and turned towards the
town.

The road to the centre was quiet, the beach empty save
for the men with the rakes patiently searching for rings and
car-keys. The bars and night-clubs on the front had with-

drawn into themselves like sea anemones at low tide as the sun, warmer now, rose steadily above the cape.

In the café opposite the station the student sat as he felt an Englishman in St Raphael should sit. A copy of *Le Figaro* lay open in front of him. He had only enough French to decipher the headlines and the captions, but that surely was enough to justify the purchase. Oh! It felt fine to sit in a café in the south of France, to have slept on the beach, to be catching a night train for Rome!

To an observer, he was obviously an alien and probably English. The garçon who brought his coffee and croissants saw a tall, rather pimply youth with skin angry where it had been exposed to the sun, and starkly white where it had not. His eyes were screwed against the brightness of the morning as it beat off the paper in front of him; his tee-shirt was bulky over his money-belt. His cut-off denims rubbed the sunburn on his thighs and his tennis shoes were torn and scuffed. The student drank the coffee, which was not as he had imagined it would be. Still, its dark and pungent essence was possibly more French even than the *café au lait* he had meant to order. The croissants were not a disappointment. He passed an hour in the café, then crossed the road to the station.

A shifting in his bowels reminded him that they had not moved since he left Dover. Anxious to establish good habits early in the holiday he glanced up and down the street and was pleased to see a sign proclaiming *Hommes* some hundred metres away. He strode purposefully towards the shady doorway. There he stopped, uncertain of how to proceed, for inside the street door of the toilet, in a small recess that somehow managed the appearance of an office, sat a woman. She was perhaps fifty, with a pleasant face and tidy appearance. She would not have looked out of place behind the reception desk of a respectable hotel. She was reading a magazine, but looked up as his shadow fell across the doorway.

'*Bonjour, M'sieur.*'

'*Bonjour,*' he responded, not wishing to be outdone. He glanced uncertainly at the sign above the door.

An uncomfortable silence was broken by the unmistakable and reassuring flush of a toilet from within. The student stepped back as a large, very French-looking man emerged from the inner room, dropped a franc into a leather bag at the woman's side and wished her '*Bonjour*' as he passed from the cool paleness of the public toilet into the street. Gaining confidence, understanding the game, the student stepped from the street into the public toilet. To his surprise the woman was on her feet, blocking his path.

'*Un moment!*'

She bustled past, an aerosol in her hand. There was a hiss, and the squeak of a damp cloth on porcelain, and another flush.

'*Voilà!*'

The student had, in fact, lost his urge to establish a good habit, but he sat in the cool darkness for a respectable length of time and paid his franc willingly.

Pondering his experience, rehearsing the detail, he strolled past the stacks of left-luggage lockers and through to the platform. St Raphael has a busy station and he had little difficulty in finding a shady spot where he could drop his rucksack and watch the world as he waited for his train. He was glad of the shade for his skin burned easily and even at that hour it was hotter than he would have liked. Still, this was the Riviera. From a pocket in his rucksack he drew a clear plastic bottle of Evian water, half full. He was not a drinking man, this student; in fact he was something of a puritan: he aspired to a simple, healthy, almost ascetic lifestyle for himself, though he was self-consciously uncritical of the mores of others. In the world but not of the world. He sipped the clean, pure water and considered once more the excellent plan he had conceived for passing the day. The train for Rome left Nice at nine o'clock that evening. Nice was an hour's journey from St Raphael, and between the two lay magical places whose names were synonymous with beauty and affluence; Juan Les Pins, Antibes, Cannes. He would alight at each one, make his way to the beach, and sunbathe and swim with the beautiful people. He would find the names proclaimed somewhere, the railway station would do if no more exotic location could be found, and pocket them with his instamatic: proof for posterity that he himself had visited, had swum, had experienced the. Riviera in all its sunburnt significance. He would withdraw untainted but enriched.

On the train he conversed in passable French with two Italian girls. He gallantly offered them his plastic bottle of mineral water and they politely declined, offering him in return a Gauloise – but he, regrettably, did not smoke. '*Merci, merci, mais je ne fume pas.*' It seemed no time till his train was pulling into the rather plain little station at Juan Les Pins. '*Au revoir, au revoir.*' His rucksack caught briefly in the door of the train as he was alighting, and the Italian girls smiled.

It was well after ten as he crossed the metal railway bridge and struck out confidently in the direction of the beach. The inscrutable sun fastened on his bare legs and arms, rendering his entry to the discreet world of the beautiful people less comfortable than it might have been. The little town was not at all like St Raphael – much quieter, almost reserved. Less commercialized, thought the student with satisfaction, for he was not a tourist but an accommodator of experiences, a serious collector of ambiances.

Perhaps he might have preferred it a *little* busier. His cut-off denims and white tee-shirt had been almost *de rigeur* in St Raphael but here seemed somehow inappropriate. Yet this was nonsense! He was a traveller, and the people of Juan Les Pins must be familiar with travellers. Still, he felt less comfortable than he had on the train, and the easy banter with the Italian girls seemed very distant.

He reached what he knew must be the last avenue before the sea, rather disappointed that he had not found a shop where a postcard could be bought. Instead of the long, sweeping promenade that he had expected there lay before him a row of expensive, dignified façades – presumably hotels. Access to the beach seemed rather limited. Perhaps further down the road? Yes, there, two hundred metres away was a side road which must surely lead to the beach. The student re-settled his rucksack on his raw shoulders and set off, with somewhat diminished confidence, in that direction.

The road did indeed lead to the beach, or a beach, for there was only perhaps two hundred metres of sand, bounded at each extremity by a concrete pier. On each pier, and on the beach, were scattered sunbeds, pedaloes and sailboards, and a staggering quantity of brown, naked people occupying themselves either actively or passively with these, like busy and contented children in a playground. The Beautiful People, for this the student knew them at once to be, were not of course *entirely* naked. Whether male or female, there was in each case a triangle of cloth, be it ever so small, across the loins. These concessions to propriety were many-hued, but the student noticed, even as he was considering whether he ought not to press on to Nice, that white was a popular colour with the ladies; black with the men.

The feeling of not belonging, which had nagged at his consciousness ever since his undignified descent from the train, was stronger now and could not be ignored. He felt confused, because this was not what he had expected, not at all. That one human being among a crowd of other human beings could feel so inappropriate, so out of context, and that that human being should be himself, baffled and un-nerved him. He was aware that he was attracting attention, that he must either retreat, or proceed with confidence. Had it been later in his month's holiday he might wisely have taken the dozen or so steps back to the relative security of the street. At this early stage, however, it seemed to him a test upon which future success and credibility depended, the first and most important challenge. Feeling slightly breathless he unslung his rucksack and made his way along the beach.

It was clear to him as he picked his way between the dazzling towels and their dusky owners that his anxiety would not leave him till he had removed his clothes. Whatever other qualifications one needed to feel at ease with this elite, nakedness, or near-nakedness, was essential. His bag full of shirts, underwear, towels and socks was a manifest absurdity, an embarrassment he could not hope to hide. He laid it down at the first clear patch of sand he could find and peeled off his tee-shirt.

The sun poured out its warmth and light on the beach, and indeed on the whole Riviera, with an even hand, but to the student it was the single spotlight of the strip-show, isolating and identifying him, hurting his eyes, making his head itch and his palms sweat, usurping rational thought and replacing it with stark, indelible images. As the stripper cannot see the faces behind the spotlight so he could not, or would not, look at those around him, whom he knew had taken note of his arrival. He fixed his eyes on a brightly coloured triangular sail that dipped and rose on the sparkling waves. He knew that he looked ridiculous as he struggled to change beneath his towel, so small and anaemic in its washed-out bluey-greens. Why was it not big and bright like the others on the beach, like the sails of the windsurfers?

At last the manoeuvre was complete, yet his near-nakedness did nothing to restore his equanimity. He felt instead as though he had played his last card, and it had proved insufficient. He was red in some parts, pink in others, white in stupid places that should have been brown. Having at last contrived to remove his clothing he now longed to cover himself up. Miserable, he stared straight ahead. A woman next to him said something to him in French. He turned. She had been lying on her back but sat up now, facing him, her brown, pointed breasts quivering still.

'Are you a guest at this hotel?'

She spoke in English now; she knew he was English. A hotel. A private beach. Behind her he saw, for the first time, the sun terrace, the open doors leading into the cool private darkness of the hotel bar, from which emerged beautiful men and women with bright, triangular cocktails in their hands. Around him his clothes lay scattered like evidence, his rucksack spilling out camera and washkit and clean shirts. Above him the white, harsh light picked him out for the entertainment of the Beautiful People of Juan Les Pins. Behind him was the sea. Tears pricking his eyes he rose uncertainly to his feet and ran, stumbling, for its sapphire anonymity, the silvery laughter of the brown, sunburnt women receding behind him as he crashed into the cold water and struck out to where the gaudy sails flicked and bobbed.

The sun, coral pink now, was dropping into an indigo sea void of sails as the night express to Rome sped through Monte Carlo. The student was comfortably settled in a compartment with two Swedish travellers who drank beer from brown bottles and conversed in guttural tones. His rucksack was firmly wedged in the net above his head and the empty plastic bottle of Evian lay by his side. An Italian phrase book was in his hand. *Acqua minerale.* The Italian for mineral water was *acqua minerale.*

DOOL

Lorn Macintyre

From a distance it looked like a mummy propped across the askew doorway. The apron, taut from chest to shins, had once been white.

Dool (Donald Macdonald) the barber was watching main street, Invernevis. The rust-eaten sheets of corrugated iron wedged between smiddy and post office looked in danger of collapsing at any moment, as if the weight of his spine on the wormed post would do it.

His left foot wasn't resting on a big black square stone. It was a surgical boot. But the calculation hadn't quite brought both feet up equal. There hadn't been anything else but barbering, since there wasn't such a thing as a built-up spade.

His arms were folded across his chest now. He wasn't waiting for custom. He knew the rotation of skulls in the village, a strict two-monthly crop. But there was a syndicate of crofters cutting each other's hair – with sheep shears, by the looks of it. As for shaving, if a hand trembled too much the legs wouldn't have usually carried it up to Dool's, and if the barber became peripatetic that was two bob extra, for the burden of the boot. But wives had learnt to shave.

So Dool wasn't waiting for a head. He wasn't waiting for anything. Main street was deserted, except for a horse that also looked bored, having been staring at dust for half an hour.

A lid lifting at his back told him his kettle was ready. He tilted it to the chipped enamel mug, then sat in his chair of

116

business, the horsehair leaking. He put the grubby towel round his neck, immersed the badger's hair brush in the mug, shook it, then began to stroke the bowl of soap.

Then he selected a razor from the shelf, pulled the blade from the long ivory handle and tested it on his thumb. He kept his hand in by shaving himself.

The enamel mug began to vibrate on the board, as if someone from the spirit world was tapping out a message, using the handle of the brush. Then the corrugated iron enclosing him began to shudder, as if it was on the move. The only steady thing in the whole shed was the razor in his fist, still pulling off soap, as the water from the mug dripped down onto his bigger boot.

The morning train from Glasgow going under the road was shaking the rusty nails from the shed. On the shelf razors slewed, one going to the very edge, the next shudder saving it. All that would come off the train would be provisions for the big house, Dool thought as he did the tricky bit between nostrils and lip. It was only April; the pleasure boat didn't start on the loch for another month.

When the wall clock righted after the train braked it told him it was going to be another long day. He couldn't sharpen the razors again; the blades were so thin that they would snap on the next jaw.

He was wiping the hairs from his nostrils on the knee of his apron when the door was pulled open, as if someone was demolishing the shed. The locals knew that there was more rust than hinge.

He saw a suitcase put down beside boots. They were laced a funny way, with sharper toes. The case was bound with a belt, with two initials slanted in a corner. Dool twisted his head. It was a W, or the case was upside down.

Dool stood up and the man sat down, leaving the suitcase by the door, as if to warn the next customer that the chair would be taken for some time. Dool was looking down on a pearl-grey hat, with a deep cleft. There was a dead leaf or something in the cleft. The hat needed a fist inside it to get it into shape.

'Wash my hair.'

It was said in a voice such as Dool had never heard, not even from those who'd come back from South Africa with imitations of the accents of the Boers they'd beaten. Dool felt like saying: say that again, just to hear the sound of it.

Instead he lifted the hat. The grey hair was parted in the middle, then swept back, tied in a tail. Dool eyed the face in the cracked mirror. If it wasn't the colour of the skin, then the mirror needed cleaning.

He was going to say: I don't do women, but the words wouldn't come out. Besides, the back of his hand had brushed the cheek. It was rough.

What Dool said was: 'You don't wash hair; it weakens it.'

'We do, where I come from,' the voice answered. The words were long, drawn out, and seemed to be delivered through the nose.

'Where is that?' Dool asked.

'Wash it, like I said.'

Dool undid the piece of cord tying it back, and ran his fingers through the hair. It felt like a fleece, straight off the sheep's back. He was doing a lot of thinking. It couldn't be an escaped convict because the prison cut was near the bone. He knew this because a local who'd wintered in a Glasgow jail had come straight off the train to ask for a prediction of growth. Dool had told him the best hair restorer was time, and advised him to keep on his cap while drinking in the Arms.

But this could be a loonie, though it didn't have the slack face and big ears of the two at the Home Farm. Best to go along with it till somebody came in, though that might not be till tomorrow. At least there were plenty of razors within reach.

Dool tilted the kettle towards the enamel mug. He'd a

good mind to scald the bugger. But he tipped the jug of cold water. Wash it? With what? He squashed the sodden bristle into the bowl of shaving soap.

Then he began to lather the head with the brush, backwards and forwards, like whitewashing a sloping grey wall.

'Now rub it in,' the mouth below the frothing white scalp ordered.

Dool dug in with both hands. He would have liked to twist the bugger's head off. There were flecks of soap all over the mirror.

'Now rinse it.'

That took a bit of thinking about. It meant putting a bucket on the floor, making the man bend his head between his knees. Dool poured the kettle over the scalp. It was a pity it wasn't boiling.

'A towel,' the customer demanded, head still down, dripping. His black boots were flecked, as if he'd walked through sleet.

Dool tossed the only towel at him.

'Now shave me,' the customer ordered, towelling his skull.

That meant limping out to the slow pump. Dool thought about going into the blacksmith's to borrow a hammer. But shaving gave him the upper hand on people. While he waited for the stove he tried to whistle.

The towel was sodden, but it had to go round the broad shoulders. He tried to tuck it in, but the collar was too tight.

'Leave it,' the customer ordered.

Though Dool's thumb found the sharpest razor, he still gave it a few slaps on the strop hanging from a hook. Then he lathered the swarthy face up to the eyes. The blade touched a cheek. The darkness wasn't dirt.

'Where do you come from?' the barber asked.

The mouth in the mirror said something, but the blade cut it away. It was rasping at the Adam's apple now. Dool

LORN MACINTYRE

looked into the blue eyes above the soap-line. It was like
looking down into deep water. Now if the blade skidded –
He tried again.

'Where did you say you come from?'

But Dool made the same mistake again, holding the
customer's nose to twist round the cheek. All he got was the
end of a word.

'From England?'

'New England.'

This fellow was too smart. Accidents could happen.

'New England is in the United States.'

Dool nodded curtly into the mirror.

'I come from Massachusetts.'

The barber nodded. He was drawing a line of soap between the nostrils and the upper lip. There was gold in the
teeth. A man in the village whose nose had got too close
to a horse spoke like that.

'M-a-s-s-a-c-h-u-s-e-t-t-s.'

It was a chant. Dool felt like stoppering the smart mouth
with the soapy brush. He held the jaw in the heel of his
hand, twisting the teeth out of alignment to get at the hairs
at the corner of the mouth. He saw the tongue and could
have cut it out. Shaving soap flopped onto the toe of his
built-up boot.

Then the mouth in his hand said something in Gaelic.
Dool stooped, putting his ear to the mouth as if it was
stopping breathing. It spoke Gaelic again. The razor
trembled.

'That's it,' Dool said, wiping away the surplus soap with
his sleeve. He showed the customer his own face in the
mirror.

'My hair's just about dry. Tie it back.' Then he said:
'Thanks.'

Dool's hand touched the hot stove.

'What kind of place is it you come from?' Dool asked.
All he remembered was Mass.

'Cape Cod's a big place.'

'Oh,' Dool said. If he could have remembered the name of the first place, he would have accused the man of coming from two places.

'It's on the Atlantic,' the man said. 'Miles and miles of shore, but a lot of fog.'

'What do you do there?'

'I'm a longshoreman.'

This time Dool had to ask.

'Shore fishing.'

'With a rod?'

The man laughed. 'With nets; big nets. For cod.'

'They're dirty fish; they won't eat them down at the big house,' Dool said vehemently.

'Cod are OK,' the man said. 'My old man was on the whalers.'

'There were men from here on the whalers,' Dool said.

'My mother had Indian blood. She belonged to the tribe the Puritans butchered. Have you read about the Puritans?'

Dool shook his head in the mirror. Reading was difficult; it wasn't something you needed at Invernevis, though he sometimes looked through a newspaper if a customer left one.

'Do you know about the *Mayflower*?'

Dool kept shaking his head. Flowers didn't interest him. You tried not to leave the road, with the boot.

'It was a boat,' the man said.

'There's a boat on the loch here,' Dool said.

'It doesn't matter,' the stranger said. 'We lived in a shack on the shore at Cape Cod. You couldn't sleep for the wind shaking it. I used to hear her praying for the old man, out there on the whaling ship.'

'What happened?' Dool asked hoarsely. The lean-to had tilted; the mirror was a pool on the river now, his boyish face peering in, wondering how deep it was while the others swam. He remembered how much he'd wanted the freedom to kick out.

'A fog came down, the worst fog they'd ever seen. It was so thick you couldn't see your hand. I told her not to worry because his ship would sit it out. We could hear their sirens.'

'Who are you?' Dool asked, trembling.

'It was such a bad fog that the whales came ashore, but the men never did. You haven't smelt anything till you've smelt a whale carcass,' he said, turning from his own reflection to confront Dool. 'She used to walk on the shore among the rotting bottle-noses, with a rag over her mouth, looking for his body. You know what I think? I think she thought one of the whales had eaten it, and when its flesh rotted – '

'Who are you?' Dool pleaded.

'I'm looking for Mistress Katie MacPhail.'

'What do you want with her?' Dool asked. He was still within reach of the razors.

'I've come a long way from Cape Cod, Massachusetts.'

'What's that place got to do with Katie MacPhail? She never once left Invernevis.'

'I'm her son.'

'There is no son,' Dool said, shaking his head with finality. 'You said it yourself; your mother's an Indian.'

'*Was* an Indian,' he corrected Dool. 'She died before the old man. He made me promise to come here and tell his first wife what had happened. He did mean to come back to her, but he got caught up in the whaling. He said to call her mother.'

Dool was not conscious that he'd picked up a razor, and that its whetted blade was pressing on his thumb. He'd been a boy at the time. Somebody from a shipping company in Glasgow had spoken in the village hall, with the laird on the platform beside him. Angus MacPhail had been one of those who'd gone forward and signed up for the promise of the new world. Dool had dreamed of going himself, but he was only a boy, short on one foot.

'My name's Angus.'

Katie had gone around telling everyone that he would be back soon, with his pockets full of money to do things to the croft. Other men had come back on leave, with silver coins they spun on their thumbs, and bits of bone from whales they said they'd killed. But none of them had any news of Angus, though Katie had kept insisting that he'd be coming home soon.

'Angus MacPhail I'm called. He spoke to me in Gaelic because he didn't want the Indian woman to understand.'

Dool remembered that morning he'd wakened up to the fog that had rolled up the loch, so thick you couldn't see your own hand. Nothing, neither wheels nor shoes had moved in Invernevis that morning. But in the afternoon the fog had rolled back down the loch, out to sea.

'Where do I find Mistress MacPhail?'

Dool took him by the arm, round the suitcase, then opened the door, gently, because there was more rust than hinge.

'You see that horse there? Go past it, then past the store. Turn up the lane and keep going till you come to the gate on the right.' He counted on his fingers. 'She's three along.'

'The third house along,' the man memorized, nodding. 'How much do I owe you for the wash and shave?' He produced a coin. 'Do you know what that is?'

'It's a silver dollar,' Dool said.

'How do you know that, if you don't know about the *Mayflower*?' the man asked suspiciously.

'I didn't say the third house along,' Dool said. 'It's the third grave along, and you don't owe me anything. There's no stone because there was nobody to pay for it.'

'When was she put up there?' the man asked hoarsely. He was standing in the doorway, his back to Dool, his hands against the doorposts. The shed was swaying.

'I can't give you a date,' Dool said. 'But it was the afternoon the big fog went back out again. She had something wrong with her stomach. They found her on the shore.'

The shop was leaning at such an angle that the suitcase fell over, onto Dool's big boot. AM, the initials said.

'You'd better come back in,' Dool advised.

He sat the man down on the chair and put the kettle back on the stove. He opened a cupboard and took out a half bottle of whisky, kept to give a dram to old bald men who came in to sit on cold afternoons, their spittles like barnacles on the stove. He tilted the steaming kettle to the two mugs, and gave MacPhail his toddy, though it wasn't cold outside. Then Dool pulled up a chair and rested his outsized boot on the shelf, among the razors.

'*Slainte*,' said MacPhail, toasting him in the mirror.

'This place, Mass – ' Dool began.

SUMMER FISH

Catriona Malan

It was hot. Bees fizzled in the over-blown roses and golden-rod blazed like bushfires. Grace stood on the brick path facing the empty house.

(*And now I will say goodbye. For the last time.*)

She held the bulk of her white bag against one hip. Thickened fingers on the dull silver key, she stepped into the shadow of the porch. Click, open, clack, and she was there. The hallway, no-man's-land and crossroads of the house, lay bright with sun. She stood, legs spangled rose and jade from the door panes, breathing the smell and peace of it.

(*I love this house.*)

As she stooped to drop her bag, colours leaped and lay on its whiteness and, momentarily, on her hair.

(*Now where will I go first?*)

Bare boards pointed in dusty rows to the foot of the stairs.

(*Up? No, I'll let it come gradually. Go round all the rooms.*)

Turn left into the lounge. A large stifling-hot room. The sun glaring in through squares and falling in dazzling oblongs in the bay of the window. Motes glittering in beams above bleached parquet.

The first thing she noticed was the shelved alcove. A tenement of soft honey-coloured wood once peopled by china figures. Attic to ground floor was abandoned. Girls, clowns, nuns, gone. And in the basement, the crystal glasses, set rim-singing at a finger stroke, were missing. She closed her eyes.

At once she heard one shrill laugh above the flat thrum of music and voices. The strangely Tibetan ring of ice on glass. She could smell the grey-blue scent of smoke. Then the room stilled. Beyond a disarray of dogs, logs sissed and puffed. The tack, tack, tack of a square brass clock, which had respectfully sung the hours, hammered the minutes flat. And from the bay window drifted the resin smell of a Christmas tree, above bright boxes, bravely dying in its jewellery.

(*Pine.*)

Its scent roused her with a tickle of unease. A feeling of something important she could not recall. The wriggle of a tiny fish in a deep pool.

(*Was it something I did? Or did something happen to me?*)

She left the room drowsing in the heat.

In the kitchen the sun was gentler. Nettles showed above the sill, the colour of the wrinkled lino. She crossed to the back door and caressed its long scars with reminiscing fingers. Seeing rigid-tailed kittens staggering and playing. Fat puppies, trusting, naughty, loved, who had ailed or aged away. The mourning. The painful discarding of battered dishes with names around the rims. She moved to the window.

Suddenly she heard clearly the pop-and-rattle of peas shelled into a bowl. The sullen flap of thick soup boiling, and the high vicious hiss of things curling in a frying-pan. Saw steam from tilted lids carry fragrance into discreetly-hung clothes above. A table had stood here. It had borne slicings, gratings, beatings and often the pliant pregnant swell of bread. Hurried happy breakfasts. Rings of damp from mugs. Letter openings, homeworks, sewing. And even deep head-down weeping. But something was wrong.

(*What is it? Something is just beneath the surface and I can't remember.*)

The little fish was rising.

Back in the hall. The stairs a pale waterfall of faded wood. Painfully she waded up, creak upon creak. She hesitated by the open bathroom door. As she went in, a large brown spider fled from his dry water-hole with faint clicks. Grace sat on the smooth beige lid. Everything was shiny, though the sun was muffled by dirty rumples of net at the window. She glanced at the steam-coloured shower curtains awry over the bath. Here two children had shrieked and splashed. Neat round bottoms and flat, unripe bodies down which foamy water slid. Leaping from bath edge to warm towels. Eggs of yellow soap. And trembling, beautiful bubbles blown floating through soapy-finger Os.

She rose and turned, fleetingly confronted by her own wan face. It slid away as she clicked open the mirrored door. Barren ribs of white shelves. Empty. Except for one red pill. Innocent as a smartie and as startling as a drop of blood. She stared in unexpected revulsion. The memory seethed but did not break the surface.

(*I'll not find it here. Close, but not here.*)

She went along the passage, treading on patterns that draughts and insects had scribbled in the dust. Without the discipline of carpets, walls seemed to trespass, still bearing the scars where frames had been. Past the children's rooms, too full of long ago to bear. Outside her bedroom door she felt the small fish dart. Roses cut from wallpaper bloomed beneath a clear finger-plate.

(*It must be here. Must be. I can feel it.*)

Flickers in the green water.

The door was ajar. It swung easily at her touch. Sunlight filled the room. It had faded the roses to grey and was painting triumphant angular splashes and shadows everywhere. The air hummed. Hopefully she crossed to sit in the curved window-seat.

(*It must come soon. I can almost remember.*)

A quicksilver flash and a ripple in the pool.

The bed-head wall was in spotlight.

(*Is it to do with love? No. I can remember that easily enough.*)

Languorous mouth-against-mouth whispers, the calm before a storm. The bend and unbend of hot backs. The intimate rub of thigh on thigh – rough on smooth. She closed her eyes.

Behind her, the window where in winter she had watched flake upon flake swither down, unable to follow one to the ground. Where summer field daisies, white as the flakes, had clung to their simple beauty. Then, deprived of freedom, had dropped minute leg-waving creatures on the sill, and browned.

Buzzing brought her out of her past. A huge bee was pacing noisily against the pane, trailing from one leg a long spider's thread. She opened the window, held the thread and let the bee weave crossly away. Now she noticed that the wild garden was cooling. She would have to go. But she closed the window again and sat down to wait for the evasive memory to come, while the bright squares slid gently on the wall.

Emptying her mind, she let pictures flicker and go at will, in all the moods and times she had lived through.

(*I can remember fun and pain and laughter and children and love. A million things. What is it that I can't remember?*)

But the little fish glinted tauntingly in its green secrecy.

At last, still puzzled, she got up stiffly and left the dimming room.

(*Let it be, then.*)

She went down, lifted her bag, leaving the colours on the floor, and shut the door behind her. Irritated. Down the warm brick path, between the roses. One last turn back. She put both hands above her eyes for this last of last looks.

There at the upstairs window a pale face was watching. Immobile.

Excitedly her fingers rummaged. Found the key. The

door banged behind her as she struggled upstairs. Creaks, shadows, dust, and weakening sunshine. Into the bedroom. No one. Nothing. She sighed. Then smiled.

(*Well, now that I am back I will stay here until I do remember.*)

After some time she heard the turn of a key, and voices loud and faint as they moved in and out of the rooms below. She did not move.

(*It is my house. I will explain why I am here.*)

Feet on the stairboards. Breaths heavy with the climb. Feet in then out, in then out of the rooms. The door opened. A short man came in dusting his fingers on his bulging waistcoat. He looked around, calling over his shoulder, 'There, you see, Madam, you must have been mistaken. This is the last room. And there is no one here.'

The tiny fish tasted air.

She remembered.

SCARAB

Ian Rankin

'Take it off.'

The Egyptian was grinning, the grin highlighting his several gold teeth.

'Take it off,' he repeated.

For as long as she could remember, Lily Devereux had worn around her neck that tiny black scarab given to her by her father, and now she was being urged to remove it, in the face of a far greater stone scarab by the sacred lake at Karnak.

'Go on, Lily,' her husband said, while the small Egyptian danced in front of them, his arms shaking.

The heat was appalling, and she wished she were back inside the cool, pillared hall of the temple, instead of out here beneath the bare, blistering sun, wilting beside a biologically dead lake and the huge stone representation of a scarab.

'My father told me never to take this off.'

They had come here to Egypt, actually, for sentimental reasons. Lily's parents had been fervid Egyptologists, and she herself had been born inside the tomb of Seti the First. Ronald and she were to visit that tomb tomorrow, walking in the dust of her violent and bloody birth of forty years before.

In the Cairo Museum they had seen many exhibits which had been excavated by her parents back in the dangerous years just after the war. In Luxor they stayed at the same shabbily genteel hotel where Lily's parents had honeymooned. And now, at the Temple of Karnak, Lily was being enticed to walk three times, backwards, round a smooth, sculpted symbol of fertility.

'But why do I need to remove my necklace?'

The gold-toothed local giggled.

'It is unlucky is why,' he said. 'Stone scarab lucky. Make you to have baby. But black scarab,' he pointed to her pendant, almost daring, it seemed, to touch it, 'not so lucky. Make you not have baby. Is well known fact that I tell you.' He eyed her more closely. 'You have children?'

Lily stared towards her husband. His face was ashen in the heat. She knew that he would rather have been holidaying on the wet, warm coastline of Scotland. Well, of course Ronald and she had wanted children, and they had tried for them. They still tried, though more stoically now on his part, and less tearfully on hers.

Lily took the black scarab from around her neck.

'It's unlucky you say?'

The man nodded vigorously. She placed the scarab in Ronald's hand.

'Backwards three times?' she said.

The man nodded again, giggling. Some other tourists nearby laughed too, enjoying the spectacle and thankful to be bystanders and not participants.

Back in their hotel room, Lily sat in front of the portable electric fan and stared at her fine gold chain with its tiny black charm. She stroked her denuded throat, pushing the scarab about the bedside-table as though probing to see if there were life still in the insect.

Ronald added slices of lemon and ice-cubes to a jug of tonic water. He stared out across the balcony, over the great slow Nile itself with its barely moving feluccas, towards the dry yellow hills beyond. Those hills had once contained the ancient lineage of Egypt, the Kings, Queens, and High Priests, and there Lily had been born, in candlelight and in the eternal coolness of Seti's tomb.

'Surely,' Ronald said now, turning with her drink in his hand, 'surely your father would have known, wouldn't he? I mean, he could hardly *not* have known.'

His face had returned to its natural ruddy hue. He looked down on the scarab in disgust and fear.

'We can easily check up on it,' said Lily. 'But after all, we only have that horrid little man's word on it.'

'And the word of his friends.'

'Yes.' She picked up the black scarab, bringer of infertility, bringer of a twenty-year agony. It could not be true.

'Ronald,' she said, 'hold me, please.'

Patrick and Celia Gambon had returned to the Valley of the Kings in 1947 to make copies of the many rows of hieroglyphs and cartouches which, even then, were showing signs of rapid deterioration. They were recognized as experts in this field, and had been talked into making the trip even though Celia was seven months pregnant when they set out from Geneva.

They travelled downriver from Cairo in the company of Hamdi Hammam, the young man in charge of the workings in the Valley. He lightened the trip through his insistence that they drink special infusions of tea and herbs, whose recipe had been passed down through the generations from his ancestor Paneb, High Priest of Thebes. These infusions would restore their already flagging strength and cool their bodies, while also serving as an aid to the expectant mother. Hamdi fussed so much that the Gambons were forced to conclude that they were enjoying themselves, and they set to work on the copying the next morning after their arrival at Luxor.

It was decided that they should work in the afternoons, the hottest part of the day. Thus they could enjoy the cold air of the tombs, leaving the warm mornings and evenings free. Soon, however, they began to labour well into the night, hoping that the work might be finished in good time for them to travel back to Cairo for the delivery of Celia's baby. They found that the oil lamps made the atmosphere of the long, narrow tombs unbreathable, and so worked by candle-light, carefully copying each row of the kingdom's history onto long sheets of rough, thick paper.

Most of the other workers in the valley were dismissed at sundown, but Hamdi insisted on staying on with his two guests. He did not tell them that he was worried about the possibility of their being surprised by the many looters who still searched the valley at night, seeking out the many undiscovered tombs with their only-too-imaginable riches.

Hamdi sat in silence on a broken slab in the tomb of Seti the First, not daring to disturb the meticulous work of the copyists. One error could mean some future misinterpretation of an entire period in the Pharaohs' history. For Hamdi, that responsibility was too much to bear. He went outside to smoke one of his loosely-packed cigarettes, its red tip and the faint glow from the cavern warning trespassers that officials were still here, guarding the tombs even into the chilled night.

A camp had been set up at the other end of the valley, and there, Hamdi knew, tea and food awaited them, but still his friends worked on. He stubbed out another cigarette and scraped a fingernail over his gold tooth. The immense walls of the valley seemed about to swallow him in his insignificance. He was about to cry out at them, when he heard the first low moan from the tomb of Seti the First as Celia Gambon went into labour.

The two men, anxious as they were, could do little but let the screams, the terrible archings of her back, and the rocking of her head take their ultimate course. Patrick wiped the hair back from Celia's brow and rubbed her hand, calming her with words. Hamdi, spellbound and horrified, could only mutter that there should be women present to help with the labour. Why had he not thought of that sooner? There should be women; this was no place for a man. Looking around, he saw that he was in Seti's frigid tomb, not the bustling adobe house of his imagination, and he giggled. Patrick looked at him accusingly, and Hamdi's eyes obediently drifted towards the floor, where two cockroaches wandered slowly in a mating-circle.

At one point, perhaps hours later, following a particularly intimidating cry, several men ran into the tomb. They carried oil-lamps and wore grimy *galabeas* of thick, pale cotton. Hamdi knew them at once for prospective tomb-robbers, but he was thankful all the same for their company, for their shared language and shared beliefs. He greeted them, and they squatted on the floor of the tomb, passing round cigarettes and waiting for that which must happen. Even Patrick Gambon accepted a cigarette, though he had never smoked before. He smiled in thanks, hurrying back to his wife's side.

Hamdi respectfully kept his back to his old friends while conversing with his new ones, but the other men strained to see what was happening at the end of the passage, making crude jokes and enjoying thoroughly this unexpected turn of events.

Many years later, his mouth full of tarnished gold teeth, Hamdi would swear that he heard the child cry before anyone else. It was a whispered affirmation, quickly replaced by the more audible and recognizable sounds of that first shock of life. Hamdi blessed the baby under his breath, and stood up. Hearing a brittle noise under his foot, he looked down and saw that he had crushed a cockroach as large as a mouse. Through a haze of candle-light and cigarette smoke, he saw Patrick Gambon coming towards him, holding the still unclean child in his hands.

'She's dead,' he said, his voice strained to a whisper, but still finding an echo in the gallery.

At first, Hamdi thought the man must be mad; the child was quite certainly alive. But then he realized that the mother, unused to childbirth, had lost her life in the creation of another. He translated this news to the looters, who murmured their regrets and their prayers. Hamdi held his breath, still thinking of the cockroach at his feet.

One of the small knot of men stepped forward, holding out something to Patrick Gambon. He spoke a few words, and Hamdi realized that the man's gift was authentic, doubtless stolen from some uncharted tomb.

'He says that this is a charm, Mister Gambon, and that if worn by a woman it . . .'

'Yes, Hamdi, I can see what it is.' Patrick Gambon stared at the child in his arms. He swallowed and, cradling his daughter, reached out with the palm of his hand for the tiny black scarab.

'Thank you,' he said. '*Shok'ran.*'

The man, bowing and smiling, went back to his friends, who were rising to leave. They called out goodbye, but the man and child were already stalking off towards the end of the tomb. Hamdi looked around him, suddenly alone, a finger touching his gold tooth, and saw the fine paintings on the walls, their colouring still alive after a thousand years of silent ingress. They had survived, he knew now, because they were not important to this life.

Ronald Devereux smoked for the first time in his life as he sat in the waiting room of the hospital. He rose occasionally to pace the floor, checking from the window that Edinburgh was still Edinburgh outside. He thought again, with some horror, that he was too old to make a good father, too old and lifeless, his heart unsteady after years of thankless pounding and surging, now when he needed it most.

He hoped Lily was all right. It was a miracle, after all, and the doctors explained that at her age it would not be an easy birth. That Egyptian with the gold teeth had been right after all. It was a miracle. But why was it taking so long? He stubbed out his fourth cigarette, a taste like bad water in his mouth. A nurse pushed open the door.

OUR LADY
OF THE PICKPOCKETS

Dilys Rose

For many hours now, no buses have left. It is because of the rains. Everywhere is mud in my town, in Villahermosa. Her name mean 'beautiful' but she is not. Tonight she is a wet black sow and the tourists are stuck in her underbelly. My people know how to wait. Angel says they are all waiting, for death, or a Greyhound bus to Texas. It is all the same to them. Many times my people will wait all night in the bus station, without speaking, without moving. They know every way to sleep, propped against the walls like sacks of beans, piled on benches, flat out on the floor. They sleep even with the eyes open. Angel say this is because they live with the eyes closed.

Tonight there is no sleeping on the floor. Sometimes Emilia, the desk-girl, takes her broom and sweeps the water to the door. Each time she sweeps, Owaldo checks through the peanut-shells and cigarette butts for coins. He finds no coins. The black water always returns. Tourists, they don't know how to wait: always they must be speaking or moving. They don't know how to do nothing. Each minute one gets up and goes to look out into the night. There is nothing to see but two or three streetlights. Each streetlight has its own cloud of mosquitoes in its halo. And under the mosquitoes, pariahs, always pariahs, picking their sores. They are waiting too, to die, or for something to die which they can eat.

In the bus station, nothing. In Brasil street is a café-bar. It has tequila, beer and coffee but Emilia don't tell the tourists a goddamn thing. She give them a rough deal. It is because they will not speak her language and she cannot speak theirs. Only money she knows. Dollars, cents, nickels, dimes. It is not enough. I know words. I don't have to spit-shine like Owaldo, day and night and no shoes on the feet.

'Madame,' I say, 'Madame?' This lady has hair like ripe maize. It swings over her face. She is drawing on a map. She draws arrows on a map. The arrows go up the page. They cross from one colour to another. The border is where the colour changes and at the border is a river. Angel has told me about this river: American farmers shoot Mexicano wetbacks like rats.

'Madame,' I say, 'Madame, where you go?' She look up at me when I speak so I smile. Angel say a smile goes a long way with gringos. Texas is a long way.

Madame sit next to a man who drums his boot heels and slaps his hands on his knees. Madame puts down her map on the bench. Beside her she has a backpack and a big skin bag. Beside the man is a backpack and a parcel.

'At least we got most of the stuff we wanted,' the man say. He pats his parcel like a pet.

Madame has one arm inside her skin bag. She bring out cigarettes, cheap Mexican cigarettes. Angel smokes only American brands. She say, 'How long can we go on like this? One trip after another, one bus station after another. Can't we even get some wheels?' Mister twist round. He is trying to see Madame's face but it is hidden in the hair.

'We can't have everything,' he say in a quiet voice, a voice for a baby, 'You know that.'

'Everything! We can't have anything. After all this time we can't even have what any peasant here can manage without any trouble!' she say.

'Don't start, Eleanor, please, I'm tired.' Mister say and turns away. Madame grabs for the matches and drops them on the wet floor. I pick them up.

'Please, Madame, allow me,' I say. I am always polite. You don't get nowhere but into the street without manners. I strike the match on my thumbnail. Angel he teach me this trick. Madame likes me now. It is enough.

Behind Mister's head I can see Angel. He is over in the corner pretending to read the newspaper but he is watching. Angel can read only photoromances. Owaldo spits on Angel's boots. The boots must shine like hub-caps for Angel. It is normal.

'Madame, Texas?'

'San Cristobal,' she say. Many many tourists go there, there and to the ocean. Villahermosa has no ocean like Merida, and no mountains like San Cristobal, only rivers in the street when it rains. San Cristobal I have seen only in posters, since first I began sleeping here the same posters. On my first night, Angel he come up to me, he share my bench and share with me his blanket. He drink Mescal and tell me about Texas. He say Villahermosa is a stinking pigsty. He say my eyes will fall out when I see Texas.

'After San Cristobal, Madame, Texas?' She points to the arrows on the map. Her finger with the sparkling rings it stop at every arrow – San Cristobal, Oaxaca, Mexico City, Chihuahua, El Paso, Texas. A long way.

'No children,' I say, 'Madame, you, Mister, no children?' 'Not yet,' she say, 'But maybe . . .' Mister make a long face. He get up and go to look for the bus again. Madame she follow him with the eyes, the way pariahs follow the trash cart. Her eyes are hungry.

'No mother, Madame, no father. No home. Only the bus station. Only ten years old, Madame.' I am eleven but ten is a good number. Madame look at me for a long time like she trying to see under my skin. When she stop looking she give me chocolate. She believe. It is enough. I know how to wait.

Mister does not believe.

'What's your game?' he say. 'Look kid, here's a dollar.

You get yourself off home.' He hold the note between his thumb and finger. His fist is tight. 'A real American dollar.' But a dollar is not enough.

'Quit snivelling, Eleanor,' he say. 'You know, all this travelling's made you flip. Here, kid.' He waves the green paper at me. It is new and crisp. It crackles like pampas grass. I keep my hand behind my back.

'No game, Mister,' I say. 'No home. Take me with you, to San Cristobal, to Texas. Please Mister?'

'This is your doing, Eleanor,' he say. 'Can't you ever use some goddamn sense and say no? Jesus, Eleanor, can't you manage more than "maybe"?'

For a long time they talk. I don't know all the words but I know what the voices say behind the words. Mister does not want to say yes but also does not want Madame to be unhappy. One minute he say, 'OK, if that's what you really want,' and then he slam his hand down on the bench. 'You must be outta your mind, you know that. You'll be wanting to take along one of those scabby dogs next.'

After more talking, Madame takes Mister's hand and whispers something which make him laugh. Then everyone is picking up their bags and running to the door.

'Mister, Madame, the bus is here!'

'OK, kid,' Mister say. 'You win. San Cristobal, yes. Texas, no. OK?'

I will ask about Texas tomorrow. Angel say one foot on the road can take you far. Everybody is happy now: I because I am on the road, Mister because he is holding Madame close, Madame because we are all together. She smiles up at Mister all the time until he fall asleep. While he sleeps, she smokes cigarettes. The lights in the bus are out and only an old woman is talking, to her chicken. All night I light Madame's cigarettes and watch her face glow in the flame. Like this, in the flame light, her face is like the Madonna in my locket. I wear the locket under my shirt.

Angel stole it for me, from the stall of Our Lady, in the market. Our Lady of the Pickpockets. Tonight she bring me luck.

But this town we have come to is so small! There is not even a bus station. And cold! Madame say it is cold because we are above the clouds. So many mountains everywhere, nothing but mountains and chapels and low white houses. It is very early. The peasants are running down from the hills to market, bent over their loads. Very poor peasants – they don't even have mules to help them. Madame thinks it is beautiful here but there is nothing for me. I don't want to carry bales of maize on my head. Owaldo's father was a peasant before he died. His back was bent like a meat-hook.

'Tomorrow, Madame, Texas?' I say.

'Cut it out, kid,' Mister say to me, then to Madame, 'What about the sleeping arrangements, have you thought about that?'

'We'll work something out,' she say, 'won't we?'

Mister stops at a guest house on a back street and goes in. He come back with the señora who is fat and ancient. We must follow her through the courtyard, very, very slowly, because she must rest on her stick after every step. It is a clean place, with flowers and fruit trees and tiles. A boy is polishing the tiles. Much work for the boy.

The señora give us a room. A room with two beds. For me alone, one bed. For this I thank Our Lady. Already Mister is taking off his clothes. He takes everything off so slowly. He groans. He tugs at his boots. He sounds like he's sick but he only wants Madame to stop unpacking and go to bed. He wants to put his head on her chest and his hands. . . . I know about these things.

'Sleep, sleep,' he calls out as if it's for sale. Madame draws the blinds. The shutters are closed but still the sun makes stripes on the walls, stripes across the big bed.

Everybody is to sleep until noon. I take off only my

shoes. I am too hungry to sleep. Instead, I listen. Each sound I can hear, alone – the señora pounding *garbanzos*, the boy beating out a rug, the cart bumping over holes in the road. In Villahermosa, from first light, I can always hear traffic and scraping and hammering from the new railway station. Maybe some day trains will run all the way to Texas without stopping.

Inside I can hear the game in the big bed. It is normal. First whispers and bed-springs creaking. Now Mister's got on top of Madame. It's begun. He's got his head in her chest, he hold her down, he hold on tight. It's like rodeo. Mister's a cowboy on a wild mare. Madame she buck but Mister hold on. He works hard not to fall off. He's breaking her in. There. He's done it. He's won. Now he snores.

We have eaten a good meal and have been to the market where Mister buy twenty peasant dresses. He is happy because I save him much money. I bargain for him in Spanish. It is almost dark and we are walking through the crowds to the fiesta. Everyone in town must be going because the streets are packed with people. Madame hold my hand. Already she is being mother to me. I can hear noise all around – music from the shows and chapel bells and guns and rockets.

'We'll talk about it later,' Madame say to Mister.

'But Eleanor, we've gotta take care of it tonight,' Mister say. Madame pretend not to hear. She throw her hair over her shoulders and point at the fireworks in the sky.

'We don't want to miss anything, do we?' She say to me. Many times today it is like this. Mister say something to Madame and she pretend not to hear.

'Eleanor,' he say, 'look at me when I'm talking to you. Listen, what if we run into trouble? What if someone thinks we're trying to abduct the child?' I do not know this word abduct.

We go round all the shows. Mostly, I try a game and they

watch. I win many prizes – cigarettes, glasses, toy animals, a key-ring. Madame buy for me a bag to put them in. Now the streets are crazy with noise. Drunk men are singing and dancing and the air smells of sausage and sweat and beer. It's like the smell of Angel's blanket, the one he share with me if I am good. Texas, Angel say, that's all you need to say.

'Mister,' I say, 'tomorrow, Texas?' Mister is not listening. He is watching the man swallow fire. I pull on his sleeve and he bends down so his face is next to mine.

'We've been through this before. Texas is not possible. You like it here don't you? It's beautiful town. We're gonna try and fix you up here, with a priest maybe. You'll get a room maybe, all of your own. Believe me,' he say, 'Texas ain't so great.'

Angel is at the market. The rains have finished in Villa-hermosa and Emilia has washed the floor. Angel is selling the prizes I brought back. And Mister's watch and Madame's rings. I take them because they give me no money, not even when I say I go with them in the big bed. It is normal. But Madame cried and Mister yell,

'You see! Even he thinks that's why he's here. Everyone thinks so. And you call him a child!'

Angel is happy to have the watch to sell, and the ring. We will eat well tonight and the next night and the next. Angel say it is better to take your skin to the market, better to swallow fire, better to steal than to starve. I can use my eyes and my good smile and I have my Madonna. Now, under my shirt, I also keep Madame's map, with arrows going all the way to Texas. It is enough. I know how to wait.

THE TRAVELLING POET

Iain Crichton Smith

One autumn day he stopped at my door. He said he was on a sponsored walk to raise money for a boy who needed medical treatment in America. He was also a poet and as he travelled, he read his poems in pubs, halls. He sold copies of them to pay for his lodgings.

He sat in the living room and took out a bag with some of the booklets that he had had published at his own expense. There were also letters from prominent people: 'Lord X thanks you for letting him see the enclosed but is sorry that he is not able to contribute to your appeal.' 'As you will understand Lady X has many demands on her resources and is sorry that she can only send two pounds at this time.'

His poems were bad. There was also a children's story about a fox which was not much better. He found out that I was a poet and asked for my opinion. I was hypocritical as usual.

It turned out that he had been in prison and that was where he had begun to write. His father had been a crane driver; his mother had been an alcoholic. He himself had been a heavy drinker but had according to himself stopped.

'When I was young,' he said, 'we were very poor. We used to beg for clothes. I have seen myself wearing girls' clothes.'

Imagine that, I thought, girls' clothes.

His wife had left him and gone to America.

'I used to be quite violent when I was young but not any more. I was in prison a few times.' This long journey to raise funds for the boy was in a way a rehabilitation for him.

He had cuttings and photographs from various local papers, with headlines such as the following: 'Ex-Convict Raises Money for Charity Mission'. And so on. He was very proud of these cuttings, and of his letters on headed notepaper, from the aristocracy, from Members of Parliament. He had even sent a copy of his booklet to Ronald Reagan, to Mrs Thatcher. I thought he had an adamant vanity.

He left me the story about the fox to read at my leisure so that I could give him an opinion on it when he returned.

As he travelled northwards he phoned me every night.

'I feel,' he said, 'as if you are interested, as if I'm in touch with home.' He discovered the luminousness of landscapes (he himself had been brought up in the city). One night he slept in a barn and when he had asked for a clock to get him up in the morning the farmer had told him, 'You have a clock. You wait.' The clock turned out to be a cockerel. 'Imagine that,' he said. He was happy as a sandboy. Another time he saw a fawn crossing the road.

'Tonight,' he phoned, 'I'm booked into the Caledonian Hotel. I shall pay for my room with some booklets of my poems.' He had already raised the almost unbelievable sum of £2000. 'I ask for cheques so that I won't be tempted to drink the money.'

He also said to me, 'I mentioned your name to the landlady but she had never heard of you.'

Actually it bothered me a little that she had never heard of me. It also seemed to me that my visitor had become more dismissive of me, more sure of himself. After all he was not a very good poet, indeed not a poet at all.

Let me also say that I wished he had not come to the door. I had my own routine. I started writing at nine in the morning and finished at four. He had interrupted my routine and also put me in the position of being hypocritical about his poems. I had met people like him before. For instance, here is a story.

145

Another poet of approximately the same calibre as my visitor had accosted me once in Glasgow. He was unemployed, his wife had left him, he had smashed his car, his father was dying of a stroke, and his mother of cancer; he had been cut by a razor when he was a bouncer in a night club; he had been charged with sexual assault; he had fallen out of the window of a second storey flat after taking drugs. Now it might be considered that such a person might turn out to be a good poet but in fact his poems were very sentimental and didn't reflect his life at all. Such is the unfairness of literature. What can you do for such people who have experienced the intransigence and randomness of the world and cannot make use of it?

My visitor disturbed me. I imagined him as I have said learning the luminousness of the world, coming across pheasants, foxes, deer; rising on frosty mornings among farm steadings; setting out in the dews of autumn; writing his poems ('I have no difficulty at all: I can write four poems a day easy'); meeting people.

One night he phoned me and said that he was going to have an interview with the Duke of —. The local paper had asked to take a photograph of the two of them together.

Alcoholism is a terrible thing. I know a talented man who is in the entertainment world and who often does not turn up at concerts etc. because he has been inveigled into taking a drink. It was really quite noble that this 'poet' was taking his money in cheques so that he would not be tempted into using it to buy drink. Drily he toiled on, changing his poems and booklets into cheques, having as far as I could see nothing much of his own at all.

I can't write. Isn't that odd? Most days when I sit down at my desk I have no difficulty at all in writing something. But from the time that this poet called on me, I have written nothing, I have dried up. I think of him plodding along a dusty road, stopping at a hotel or a boarding house, negotiating with the sharp-eyed owner, paying for his keep with pamphlets, poems. What a quite extraordinary thing. Nevertheless I should have had nothing to do with him. And I am paying for it now. This is the first time I've ever had writer's block. What does it mean?

Maybe he won't come back. He hasn't phoned so often recently and when he does he sounds more independent, as if the two of us were equals.

Last night he phoned. He had run into another writer in a pub. This writer decorated the wall of his room with rejection slips. He didn't think he was getting fair treatment because he was a Socialist. He dressed in a Wild West outfit. He was 'quite a character'. 'Listen,' I nearly said to my visitor, 'don't be deceived by him. He is a bad writer. I can smell his amateurism a mile away. People like that always dress in an outré manner, they always say that they are not understood. Avoid him. Listen to me instead.'

I started writing when I was about eleven. I believe that routine, hard work is the most important thing in any art. I sit down at my desk every morning at nine. Without a routine all writers and artists are doomed. I have never been an alcoholic. Writing is my life: that must be the case with all artists.

I should have asked him how he had got involved in his walk to raise money for a boy who is dying and is to be sent to America where the 'poet's' wife is. Maybe she left him because he didn't make any money, because he insisted on taking part in such outlandish projects. On the other hand she might have left him when he was in prison. 'They were very good to me in prison. It was there I met the man who illustrated my booklet. I had five hundred printed. Who is your publisher? Do you think you could interest him in my poems, my story about the fox?'

A startling statement he had made was, 'This is all that I have left, my writing.'

When I was younger I actually used to taste the excitement of art. I remember days when myself and my current girl-friend would travel on a green tram in Aberdeen. Mornings were glorious. I used to shout out lines from Shakespearean plays in cemeteries, among the granite. 'The great poet,' I used to say, 'is always on the frontier.'

Later I went back to Aberdeen and had the following fantasy. My earlier self met me on the street wearing a student's cloak. He was with a group of his friends. They passed me in the hard yellow light laughing, and probably never even noticed me. Perhaps they thought of me as a prosperous fat bourgeois. My earlier self didn't recognize me but I knew him. He was as cutting and supercilious as ever.

I don't think my visitor will visit me on his way south. He hasn't phoned for a week now. He is probably lost in admiration for his genuine artistic friend who is so daring. I feel sorry for him. Really he's so innocent with all his talk of cockerels, barns, deer. I am sure he will have another copy of the story of the fox and not ask me for my opinion. Perhaps his companion has heard of me, dismisses me.

Once before my wife left me I saw a small knot of weasels, a mother weasel with her tiny family, crossing the road. They looked like notes in music.

Another thing I have discovered about myself, I hate the cold. And the rain.

Autumn is passing and he hasn't come. I have heard nothing more of him, Perhaps he did after all use some of his money for drinking. Perhaps he has returned to prison. Perhaps he went berserk one night, was arrested. It is not easy to travel alone, and one's wife to be in America. There is no such thing as goodness: aggression must out. The greater the creativity the greater the aggression if thwarted.

It is winter. There is snow on the ground, he certainly won't come now. And I have not written anything for two months. I begin to write and I fail to continue. The reason my wife left me was that she said I didn't speak enough to her, about ordinary things. As a matter of fact I found that I couldn't speak about ordinary things: I would try to think of something to say but couldn't.

Listen, let me tell you a story which I read in some book or other. There was a mathematician in Cambridge who knew that being over forty he could no longer do original work in his field. So he spent his time making up cricket teams to play against each other. One cricket team would have names beginning with B such as Beethoven, Brahms, Balzac. Another one would have names beginning with A such as Joan of Arc, Aristotle, Archimedes. One day he received a letter from India which contained a number of incomprehensible equations, and he threw the letter into the wastepaper basket. However in the afternoon he usually went for a walk with a friend of his (also a mathematician) and he told him about the letter and the equations. The result was that they retrieved them from the wastepaper basket. It turned out that they had been created by a young Indian genius who had never been taught orthodox mathematics. He was taken over to Cambridge and died young. It is said that his last words were, Did you notice that the number plate on the ambulance was a perfect cube?

Now I'm sure that man had no small talk.

Who in fact is the boy and what disease is he dying of? Maybe my visitor faked the whole business in order to make money. But no, I don't think so: the story is true. He showed me a newspaper cutting which described the boy but I didn't read it very carefully. I have difficulty with detail and especially with people's names.

He must by now have collected £3000 with his bad poetry. What an extraordinary thing.

Actually up until the very last moment I didn't believe that my wife would leave me. I used to say to her, You won't find anyone else as interesting as me. She picked up her case and took a bus. And never said another word to me. I waited and waited but she never phoned. I tried to trace her but was unsuccessful. She was quite beautiful: she will find someone.

Actually she used to weep over stories on the TV. She would dab at her eyes or run to the bathroom. At first I didn't realize what was happening.

Every night I gaze up the road before I lock the door. I am waiting for my poet but he never comes. He has become a mythological figure in my mind like the Wandering Jew. His bag is full of undrinkable cheques. His mouth is dry. He cannot afford the money for the phone. All the money that he collects he puts in his bag which swells out like a balloon. Maybe that's it, he can't afford to phone.

Or he has gone home.

Or his wife has come back to him.

Or he has shacked up with his Wild West friend.

Or he has become so stunned by the beauty of the Highlands that he will never leave them again.

And here I am making money out of his wanderings. By means of this story. Whereas he . . .

I imagine the boy in a hospital in America. He is being watched over by doctors, surgeons. They are all looking at a clock. 'Soon he will come with the money,' they are saying to the boy. 'You must trust him. Till then we can't treat you.' And he swims across the Atlantic with his bag of cheques. He fights waves, he pacifies the ocean with his bad poems. Out of the green water he coins green dollars. And the boy's breathing becomes worse and worse and the doctor says, 'He won't be long now.'

It has begun to snow. He is perhaps out in the snow in the Highlands, perhaps at John O'Groats with his bag. The snow is a white prison round him: he can't even take a nip of whisky. I feel sorry for him. He should come in out of the cold, he has done enough. He has had more courage than me. With his bad poems he has done more than I have with my good ones. I can see that. And he was just as poor as me.

My writer's block has persisted. I think I am finished as a writer.

The snow is falling very gently. A ghost tree clasps the real tree like a bridegroom with a bride. They have had the worst winter in Florida in living memory.

What a sky of stars. And yet I see them as if I was a spectator. I'd better shut the door, he'll never come, my muse in her girl's dress will never come again. I shall have to take account of that.

I heard a story today about a villager. He has run away with a woman much younger than himself and left his wife. It is said that he was the last person anyone would have expected to have done anything like that. What does he hope to gain? What energy, what a strange leap. Will there not come a time when he will make a third spring and then a fourth one? As if Romeo and Juliet were still alive . . .

Last night I thought I saw him emerging out of the snow with his bag. When I went to the cat's dish there was a snail eating the food. Unless I take my bag on my shoulders I shall never write again. Unless I am willing to accept the risk of bad poems.

The phone rang but it was a wrong number.

Imagine first of all surviving in girl's clothes and then in bad poems.

I am sure that when the spring comes he will be happier. I can almost hear the ice breaking, the sound of running waters, the cry of the cockerel. The fox shakes itself out of its prison of snow. Meagre and thin. It laps at the fresh water. All around it is the snow with its white undamaged pages.

CONFESSION AT ALTITUDE

Alexander McCall Smith

He remembered the first time he had made the trip. He had done it stand-by then, anxiously awaiting the humiliating last-minute boarding, flying by the seat of the pants. It was different now. He could travel first class, booking a seat at the last moment, making the return journey whenever he wanted. It was a new league of comfort. Stewards were at his beck and call. Nothing was plastic. Wine glasses were filled from full-sized bottles of wine; the coffee was served in bone china; the seats went all the way back.

To begin with, he felt vaguely guilty. He was not really given to luxurious living. As a rule, he disliked plush restaurants and expensive hotels, finding something dangerous, almost obscene in their seductive materialism. His reaction, as he had become wealthier, had been to live a plainer rather than a more elaborate life. This expensive form of travel was his only real luxury, his only real self-indulgence.

The flights to America were business trips. Ten years ago, shortly before his thirtieth birthday, he had discovered – or stumbled upon, as he thought of it – a talent for the writing of film music. It had been a radical departure for him. He had been perfectly comfortable in his position at the music school, teaching harmony to students of varying degrees of talent. He had also found the time to do a certain amount of composition himself. There had been two symphonies that had been performed twice and then ignored, and these had been followed by a few minor pieces commissioned for obscure festivals. People had been encouraging about his work, but he was sufficiently realistic to appreciate that it was mediocre. He was not a good composer, at least not of serious music.

Then there had been the meeting with an academy contemporary with whom he had lost touch. He had been persuaded to try his hand at writing a short piece for a minor feature film – a commission accepted by his friend, who had then realized that it was impossible for him to find the time to do it. He agreed to accept it and he found that he enjoyed the task immensely. Rather to his surprise, the producer of the film was delighted with the result. Further commissions arrived and were equally successful. After a year, he was faced with the dilemma of choosing whether to stay in his post, with its pension and its predictability, or to become a freelance composer of film scores. He chose the latter, feeling like a man who was staking a year's salary on a racehorse.

His wife had supported his decision. She was a teacher of the violin and her earnings, although small, would be able to see them through the uncertainties of the transition. When, after two months, the work temporarily dried up, she had taken further pupils. The hitch, though, was temporary: a major commission soon arrived, this time from Los Angeles. It was for a big film, a crass film, which, like most such films, was bound to be lucrative. A record was issued of the sound track, and through the tenacity of his agent each time this was bought he earned a royalty. He was now comfortably off. He turned down commissions he felt lukewarm about, accepting only those which caught his imagination. There was no shortage of these.

All the time his wife continued with her pupils. She could have stopped teaching, but loyalty lay bone-deep within her and she insisted on guiding them through the perilous shoals of their music examinations. Then there would be younger brothers and sisters waiting for their time to learn the violin and these too would be taken on.

Like a missionary sticking to her post, she sat in her music room in their rambling Edinburgh house and listened to middle-class children scrape and whine their way through the classics. She was often alone now, as he would be away in London or Los Angeles, meeting his producers, talking to the cynical, shallow men who manipulated the candy floss of mass entertainment.

Then, on the way back to the airport in Los Angeles, in a limousine owned by a film company, one of his producers said to him:

'Jack. I never asked you this. You got a wife back in Scotland?'

'Yes.'

The producer looked thoughtful. 'Look. Next time you come across, bring her. We'll pay. You, me and Louise can go up to the mountains for a weekend. No business talk. We'll just sit and look at the rocks and have a good time.'

She had taken little persuading. There were a few arrangements to be made in order to free her from her pupils, but she succeeded in clearing her diary and he made the bookings. He had to be there to discuss the finishing touches to a score he had been working on for six months. It was another block-buster and they were all pleased with the way the music had worked out. It was as if he had within him an endless well of memorable, superficial melodies.

They drove to Prestwick and left the car at the airport. They were to fly to New York, where they would stay for two days before going on to Los Angeles. He had no business to do in the East, but he thought it would be pleasant to spend a short time in Manhattan. He wanted to take his wife to the Rainbow Room, to listen to the black jazz band and to dance fifty storeys above the streets, watching the tiny yellow cabs crawling below and the people like scurrying ants.

Although it was mid-summer, the flight was virtually empty in the first class. Between them and the next passengers there were two vacant rows of seats, leaving the cabin staff standing by idly, waiting for any opportunity to perform some small service for their charges. They downed a glass of champagne shortly after take-off and then tackled a rich and carefully prepared lunch. She drank three glasses of wine – far more than she was accustomed to have. He drank four, but felt no ill effects. The wine was deliciously smooth claret, the sort of wine he knew would never disagree with him.

Afterwards, when the empty coffee cups and the untouched petit-fours had been removed, they reclined their seats and paged through magazines. She read a copy of a glossy society monthly.

'Look,' she said, pointing to the Diary, 'this woman does nothing but go to dinner parties and weddings.' She read him an extract from the litany of names. Everybody was 'delightful' or 'dear' or 'charming' and lived in 'exquisite' or 'exciting' homes.

He listened, but did not really take in what she said; it was a long time since they had talked. He was reading a business magazine. He admired businessmen and their world. They made plans, took risks, changed the physical world. There was a brotherhood of them, a vast international network of entrepreneurs who understood one another. He met them casually in airports and hotels. They tended to strike up conversations by saying things like, 'Who are you with?' He found it difficult to say he was with nobody. Sometimes he said that he was with Universal Studios, which was true in a vague sense, and they were impressed. But he couldn't really talk to them.

He looked out of the window. Beneath them, like a table top of damask, was a field of cloud. Above, tinted by the protective perspex of the window, an echoing, empty sky. Far away, beyond the tip of the wing, was the vapour trail of another aircraft, a thin pencil stroke of white against the blue.

He let the magazine slip off his lap and onto the floor. The air was just the right temperature and the cabin was filled with light. Somewhere, in the back of his mind, was a line he had read about travelling into the sun. 'Born of the sun, they travel towards the sun.' He remembered it but could not recall where it came from, certainly not at altitude, mellowed by wine, half way across the Atlantic. He dozed, allowing his mind to drift idly.

Quite suddenly they fell. The plane, its nose dipping sideways, seemed to plummet from the sky, as if slipping out of the broad hands of air that had been supporting it. Inside their cabin, a trolley laden with bottles somersaulted, travelling sideways through the air to crash against the side. One of the passengers, who had been standing towards the front of the cabin, shot upwards, arms flailing, struck the ceiling and then slumped down. A stewardess screamed, clutching for support, staggering as the floor bucked beneath her.

He awoke, feeling the pressure of his seat belt pushing against his stomach, his head jerking painfully. For a few seconds he was unaware of his whereabouts; then he remembered and he thought, quite clearly, we're crashing.

He turned to his wife. She had grasped at his arms and had closed her eyes so tightly that her face was distorted by the effort. Her mouth was open, the chin and neck muscles taut.

He thought: We're over the Atlantic. In a minute, perhaps two, we'll be down. It'll be over. Dead. Dead.

He turned to her again. She had opened her eyes now and was staring at him, horrified. He returned her gaze, speechless, his neck aching, his stomach a cold knot within him. He looked into her eyes and noticed that she was crying. Again the plane gave a lurch and there came the fresh sound of crockery breaking. He stared beyond his wife's head, through the window. They were at a strange angle to the base of clouds, diving down, out of the sky.

He thought: It'll be quick now. We'll die together. Let it be quick. No impact. Nothing. Darkness.

His wife was trying to say something and he struggled to put the other thoughts out of his mind in order to listen to her. She was telling him how she had always loved him. That was all.

He looked into her eyes and thought: My music's cheap. There's nothing there. This is all that counts. And I've failed. He closed his eyes. The violent movement seemed to have stopped but the plane was still shuddering. They couldn't have much time left. He kept his eyes closed as he spoke.

'I'm sorry. I love you too.' He was counting the words now. How many more would he have the time to say? 'I let you down. I was unfaithful. I'm sorry. I had an affair. It's over. I really love you.'

He opened his eyes. She was looking at him, smiling.

'It doesn't matter,' she said. 'It doesn't matter.'

The shuddering had stopped and he realized that the horizon had returned to its normal place. The plane was still in the air, in one piece, the clouds still thousands of feet below them.

A disembodied voice reassured the passengers while the cabin staff bustled round the compartment, attending to the damage. The passenger who had been thrown into the air lay stretched out on the floor; a doctor had volunteered himself and was comforting her. The rehearsed ritual of flight was reasserting itself.

He undid his seat belt and leant forward. As he did so, his wife put her arm around his shoulder.

'I'm glad you told me,' she said. 'I didn't know, but I'm glad you told me.'

He buried his head in his hands, wanting to be ill. Rising to his feet, he left her and made his way to the bulkhead toilets. Aftershave lotion and cologne had trickled across the surface of the walls and the spicy smell of perfume was overwhelming. He dropped to his knees, his head over the stainless steel, reeling.

He got up and washed his face. One of the bottles of cologne was lying half empty on the basin and he picked it up, splashing some of the cold liquid on his brow. Then he raised his eyes to the mirror and looked at his reflection.

'Liar,' he whispered. 'Half-truth teller.' He dropped his gaze and then looked up again. About to die, he thought, right up against death, almost there, and you couldn't make a proper confession. Scared to speak.

He turned away, slipped the catch on the door and made his way back to the seat.

'Are you all right, sir?' a stewardess asked. 'I've never seen turbulence like that. Never.'

'I'm fine,' he replied. 'No damage.'

He was back at his seat.

'I want to tell you something,' he said flatly, not looking at his wife. 'A clean breast.'

She reached towards him and held his hand lightly.

'No,' she said. 'Don't. You've told me. It's over. Finished. I don't want to talk about it – ever. I still love you. I told you that.'

He was quiet. He could not go on with it. Silence. He looked out of the window and watched the distant, precious clouds. In his mind's eye he saw the other's face, the face of his folly, his unfaithfulness. A beautiful face, haunting, almost feminine – almost like the face of a woman.

THE SNARK
WAS A BOOJUM

Ian Spring

*They roused him with muffins – they roused him
  with ice –
They roused him with mustard and cress –
They roused him with jam and judicious advice –
They set him conundrums to guess.*

LEWIS CARROLL

Laertes Lebrun, the great French detective, sat silently, resolutely applying a very special pomade to his moustaches with a fine-toothed tortoiseshell comb. Here he was – ensconced alone in his room at Cathay, the country house of the Cholmondeley family, a various estate of sundry pieces that glowed vaguely in that limbo of opulence and indecision that Lebrun knew was what he saw as perpetually English. But this was not the Lebrun of yesteryear. Aged, enfeebled, inflicted with or affecting an infirmity that severely restricted his mobility and confined him for the best part to a cumbersome bath chair. When Wisden, the English country doctor and old friend of Lebrun, arrived after such a long absence from his erstwhile companion, he would be shocked: the hairs of Lebrun's moustaches had bolted – suddenly they were quite cadaverously white.

There was no doubt that at Cathay the Cholmondeley family were accommodating in the care of their guests. There were the simple pleasures of English country life applied with a panache that had once appealed to Lebrun. The finest nuances of his taste were catered for. In the

159

morning when he arose, there sat attendant on him a bowl of warmed, slightly salted water and a dish containing some white powder for cleaning his teeth. In the evening before he retired a bowl containing exactly three tablespoons of olive oil – which he favoured for the care of his moustaches – sat upon a steel tripod heated by a single smokeless blue paraffin flame. In the patio the chaise-longue was arranged at an angle that pleased him as he sat nourished by the mid-morning sun. All things leaned towards convenience – and yet for Lebrun at that time, there was no *commodité*. An ultimate weariness assaulted him.

At seven o'clock the manservant came to enquire his pleasure.

'Port or claret, Monsieur Lebrun?'

'Claret, if you please, *un soupcon*', Lebrun replied.

'Medoc, St Emilion or Graves, Monsieur?'

'Medoc.'

'Pauilac, Margaux, Saint-Julian or Cantenac, Monsieur?'

'Pauilac.'

'Chateau Lafite, Chateau Latour, Chateau Mouton-Rothschild, Chateau Pichon-Lalande, Monsieur?'

'Chateau Lafite, *s'il vous plaît.*'

'Nineteen-seventeen, nineteen-eighteen or nineteen-nineteen?'

'I will have the seventeen. *Merci!*'

Lebrun's soul signed with a misery at this capricious test of his discrimination. It was a strange design that condemned him to this – that his life revolved around an eternal series of increasingly refined choices. Lebrun felt totally divorced from his fate – as if some enigmatic god had imposed this life upon him. The insistent questions, the endless quest towards some catharsis of perfection. He had once thought that he understood the pattern to probe the mysteries of life. The Puzzle, the Quest, the Shaping, the Solution. Flurries of little grey cells endlessly reforming themselves to an infinitely complex formula until the moment of joy – the exact configuration! The Key to fit the Lock. The mystery unlocked. *Was* the art of the detective like this? Some sequence of discrete choices. Perhaps it was so. And he had always taken the right road, always pared the filament of truth from the body of fiction or fancy. Always, until now! And now the weight of age and infirmity and experience held him down.

Lebrun was old. He was not, however, moribund. There was nothing deathly in his thoughts. He who had delved so often into the consequences and ramifications of death had come at this age to some impasse. Now for the first time he was uncertain. He was unnerved by the final mystery. As never before he was in expectation of something other than a meaningless vacuum beyond the veil. Lebrun was old, but he had not lapsed into indifference. Lebrun the pristine philosopher did not quite know why he was here, suspended in this place, and yet for Lebrun the Detective there could be only one unavoidable purpose. Lebrun, the greatest detective of this or any other age, could only be here at Cathay to *solve some mystery*! However, if this was so then there was an inconsistency. Lebrun knew of no crime committed at Cathay – although the place had an aura about it, perhaps the ghost of some evil act that had taken place there. If there had been a crime committed there were no suspects – Lebrun could not remember meeting any of the guests or the staff at Cathay. The mystery was more recondite than any he had ever known, for this time there was no crime, no suspect, no prognosis, no *solution*. This time he was asked not only to solve the conundrum but to *postulate the question itself*. The starting point, he realized, must be the clues. There must be clues and clues upon clues – for any vestige of experience or reality could be a clue. The best clues, of course, were those that were never titled as such, that passed idly by as footnotes to the great text. Lebrun, of course, had the touch that delivered these insubstantial pieces of the puzzle. Hopefully, he could redeem himself and unearth enough shards to reconstruct the whole piece, and finish the job.

So Lebrun searched, and Lebrun found clues – almost with ease. In each of the several rooms some enigma seemed to present itself. In one a chessboard set correctly for the game but with one piece missing – the king's pawn black. In another a singular coincidence startled him – a dark red blotch on a desk blotter seemed to conform to a perfectly symmetrical image of his own moustaches. In the pink room he noticed side by side, between Watt's *Latin Grammar* and a home counties gazetteer, two copies of *De Nugis Curialium* by Gualteri Mapes, edited by Thomas Wright, similar in composition but different imprints. The task was tedious but Lebrun persisted until he revealed the lacuna of the first of the volumes set against the second. The single sentence read: *And these insubstantial beings are of a nature betwixt Man and Angel and cannot, by dint of their own constitution, succeed to the House of their Maker.* Not the words but the tone of the passage brought a sudden chill to Lebrun's composure. Eventually, in the green lounge, Lebrun found something that seemed to him a singular oddity. A book of verse open at a page of the poem 'The Hunting of the Snark' by Lewis Carroll. At the top of the page was scrawled in red ink 'The Five Unmistakable Marks of the Snark'. Glancing through the poem he noted the five unmistakable marks:

1. was its taste (which was meagre and crisp);
2. was its slowness in taking a jest;
3. was its fondness for bathing machines;
4. was its habit of getting up late.

The fifth and final unmistakable mark of this strange beast was inexorably deleted from the leaf in black Indian ink. No amount of scratching could reveal that fatal clue.

The setting of the sun that evening passed by unnoticed by Lebrun, engaged as he was in his labours. Reluctantly he called his ruminations to a halt for that day. Wisden would arrive that night but his aged comrade would retire before then. He decided to spend a half-hour before his night-cap to pen a letter to his friend. He concluded –

> My very dear Wisden, it has been so long. I hope that my short summary of the enigma that is presented to us will stimulate your curiosity. Finally, I say to you two things that you may think on tonight. Firstly, I hope that you have met our friend the waiter. Secondly, consider the conclusion of the poem of the snark – *mais en Francais*! A very good night and may le Bon Dieu preserve you until the morning, my dear Doctor.

> Your true friend,
Laertes Lebrun.

Lebrun knew that amongst all the confusion and uncertainty he was close to an answer. His old bones knew the feeling too well. Wisden, his old friend and confidant, would arrive in the morn and would be faced with a revelation. Objectively projecting his intellect outwith himself, Lebrun prepared to wait calmly for the outcome, curious in anticipation of the concluded labours of those tiny grey cells that he had always lauded. They were his private army, peopling his private universe – each living and dying on an impulse. They would come good. To each problem there was a solution. Thus he retired to a feverish sleep.

*   *   *

In the morning much had changed. No one attended Lebrun that morning at Cathay. His fever had resolved to a pallid mask that hid untold woes. He knew that he was obliged to outline the concluding details of the puzzle to his friend Wisden. After the accepted pleasantries, this he did in his usual concise but teasing fashion.

'And now, *mon cher ami*. I see from your baffled expression that it is necessary for me to elucidate.' Lebrun

163

composed himself but some may have detected a shift in his usual confident posture.

'You must understand that my reluctance is simply because the truth may be painful to you as it is to me.'

'Nevertheless, it is the truth.'

There was a taut silence for a moment.

'The truth, my dear friend, began to come through to me last night with a sudden realization. It was this. I, the great Laertes Lebrun, was weary. Not only weary, but I was struck with a strong sense of futility! There seemed no end to the thankless task I had assigned myself – to decipher the clues I had discovered in my seeming eagerness.'

'Mon ami, *ambition*, it is the fifth mark of the wretched snark. I, Laertes Lebrun, was too ambitious. It was when I abandoned my beloved logic and relied instead on my *intuition* that the solution came.'

Lebrun paused, almost as if to ascertain that the pieces did fit before revealing the inevitable.

'Think, Wisden. 'The Hunting of the Snark' – it is what you call in English the nonsense poem. It is exactly that – it makes *no sense. Do you not see*! The impossible snark, the bibliographical importunities of Monsieur Wright, they were, how do you say it . . . what you call it . . . the *red herring*! We were, how do you say it, *duped*. I, the great Laertes Lebrun, the finest detective of all time, was fed like a goose!

'And yet, if you think of it, my friend, what is the *red herring*? It does not exist in real life. It is a product of fiction for it presupposes an intention to deceive – the design of another intelligence. The device of the omnipotent author!

'To deceive or to tease. The missing chesspiece – I was a pawn in this game, of course. The blemished blotter that parodied my own moustaches. But the solution, my dear Wisden, was in none of this. It was to be found in something much smaller.'

Lebrun sighed; a long deep sigh that billowed in the terse air with all the desperation of his perhaps non-existent soul. The realization came upon him that his last case, his final answer, was his greatest triumph – but the solution was harsh and bitter and afforded him little pleasure.

'My dear Wisden,' he recommenced, but Wisden was no longer there. 'The solution is in the *cedilla*! I asked you, you remember, to look at the end of the nonsense poem – *mais en Francais*! You remember the end. Where the silly creatures are hunting everywhere for the baker:

> They hunted till darkness came on, but they found
> Not a button, or feather, or mark,
> By which they could tell that they stood on the ground
> Where the Baker had met with the Snark.

Here are the notes you yourself have scribbled, my friend. *Ils ont cherché ca et la . . .* Your French, of course, like all the English, is intolerably clumsy, but it is sufficient to see the point – *C'est ne pas ca*! I, Laertes Lebrun, master of many tongues, asked him for *un soupcon*, and he in his imperfect tongue replied to me – *un soupcon, Monsieur*! Lebrun paused to gain a faltering breath.

'The humble cedilla. A small thing but conscpicuous by its absence. And why . . .?'

Lebrun cast his eyes around him for a cue, but there was none.

'It is the English typewriter – a crude instrument at best – it has not the cedilla!'

'Do you not see? Our words are merely these inconsequential markings on a sheet. We are ourselves a fiction! Creations of another's imagination!'

Lebrun was all alone now in a vacuum. The greatest detective that was ever in creation had, as he was fated to do, solved the great enigma – the ultimate problem of his own existence. He reflected that there was no choice. It had been inevitable that before his end he would fathom these depths – otherwise he would never have been created; for as much a part of his make-up as his moustaches, his fastidious concern for order, was his infallibility. Lebrun had never failed. He had been teased all along but he had not been defeated. However, there was no choice now – as it had been all along. As much as anyone he was a prisoner of his own created self. The weariness in his bones no longer troubled him. His infirmity was a pretence of a kind – the artist's final chiaroscuro. His now was the fate of Carroll's baker: to out in mid breath with the hint of a cry – a futile last gasp for his individual existence.

Now? There was a great variety of poisons and mediums. Mere water now, he knew, could act as arsenic blessed by the flashing rod of the fictional ghost – the philosopher's stone that could transmute lead into gold, transfigure bread into flesh, pen reality into fiction. But that was not the chosen road and, reflecting gratefully that there were no more decisions after this one, Lebrun straightened his posture, carefully lifted the pistol the gracious curve of which had automatically been drawn in his right hand, determined to take pleasure in his last eternal moment in this sphere of his existence, and, almost silently, shot a hole neatly, with careful symmetry, in the centre of his forehead.

HENRY'S BOTTOM DRAWER

Valerie Thornton

There's Lizzie and Mac the Chef and Mrs Dorrie and Flora.

Lizzie's the odd one out, being from the mainland, from the south as they say. She has long black greasy hair, devastating acne and no teeth. Her nose is slightly hooked and she is known as the witch. She spends all day washing pots in one of the kitchen sinks, and if anyone baits her she acts wild and threatens them with a kitchen knife. Sometimes someone teases her in a kindly way and she laughs garishly, her toothless mouth wide, her eyes imploring you to find her attractive. Robbie the kitchen lad once concealed a foil-wrapped match-head in her cigarette and when it exploded clean across the kitchen she screamed and laughed alternately for at least five minutes. She refuses to say how old she is, but she can't be more than twenty-five.

Mac the Chef looks like a bull – broad forehead and curls – and spends his afternoons, between lunches and dinners, lying on a narrow bed up the back stairs conducting Radio 3. He lives in a cramped caravan in Kirkwall with his kids and a pregnant wife. Food no longer interests him. He carries a fetherlite in his pocket and dreams of vague symphonies.

Mrs Dorrie, the breakfast cook, has a big face on a small dumpy body. She meanders in late every morning, while irate early-ferry passengers take it out on whichever of the waitresses are up. There is always a suggestion of spirits in the air when Mrs Dorrie is near you, but her heart's in the right place. She's even kindly to Henry.

Flora, the head waitress, is tiny and bottle-blond, with a beehive. She swoops on all the chance tables, the ones that tip, before anyone else can get to them and haws professionally into their wine glasses, behind the swing doors, before polishing them with a napkin. You daren't show disapproval, any more than you dare go for a chance table.

None of the punters out front ever sees Henry. He's kept to the kitchen and given the worst jobs like peeling the potatoes – a morning's work with a knife and cold sharp water. Mac the Chef ignores him, but Lizzie screeches abuse at him, because he alone is below her in the pecking order.

Teenie's the other permanent waitress, living in and sleeping in every morning for breakfasts. They send one of the chambermaids to call and call outside her door. Her father's a lighthouse keeper on the Skerries and Robbie the kitchen lad fancies her. She has long blond curls like a fairy princess and exhales her cigarette smoke up and down in a sweeping shaft like a searchlight.

The boss likes tripe, but you never see him, while his wife drifts around pretending to count the biscuits. That's about everyone, except for Henry, or Henrietta, as Lizzie calls him.

No one knows how Henry came to be here, unless he's been thrown out of every other hotel in the country, but he's a long way from home – London – and a longer way from any kind of peace.

He's not been here long. Long enough to be banned from all the local pubs and hotels. But then it doesn't take Orcadians, or any other islanders, long to show an outsider that his idiosyncrasies are not tolerated. He really ought to have stayed in London, though. There's lots more like him there, aren't there?

This morning he looks like any other kitchen worker,

hunched meekly over a vat of filthy potatoes. He's got blue national health specs, stringy beige hair, a blue pullover and beige crimplene trousers.

It's only when you look a bit closer you see the side fastening on his trousers. But you'd never spot that if it weren't for his watch, which could after all be borrowed from his sister. Or maybe his bare arms give him away but then it could be alopecia, except that he has finely plucked eyebrows and a fairly heavy shadow on his face. No, the real giveaway is when you pass behind him. There, in the gap of back between pullover and trousers, is the un- mistakable waistband of a pair of tights. Maybe he's cold. Maybe, like the watch, they're borrowed from his sister. Maybe not. Henrietta right enough.

But so what? Why not? Why shouldn't he wear what he wants? He's not harming anyone, is he?

But the next morning when you first see him with his blond wig and padded bra, it's a bit disconcerting. He knows it too. He looks at you with his blue eyes, over the top of his blue specs, and tells you all about it. His man's lips look odd moving the pan-sticked stubble, but his eyes are real. He tells you how people spit on him and beat him up. How they're always throwing him out of a job, although he works hard and unprotestingly at the worst jobs. He's forty-six. And he's been in the wrong body since he was born. He knows he's a woman. He knows he feels like a woman. But no one will let him be one.

What must it feel like to have these weightless spaces strapped to his chest? He's such an incongruous woman too, with his big raw hands and man's nails. His face isn't even pretty. It's imploring for delicacy to be read in the deeply etched male lines, begging for an illusion of downy peach skin from the clogged stubble. He must be genuine. No one else could bear to look so grotesque. And, more's the pity, he'd make quite a nice little man, if he wanted to.

He accepts Mac the Chef's icy rejection with humility,

and allows Lizzie's torrents of incoherent spitting abuse to fall unheeded around him. The boss's wife's shifting gaze always drifts away from him and the summer waitresses giggle behind their hands at him. He sees it all, and reads it as a measure of the success of the illusion.

He knows he shouldn't go to the dance. But his tiny skylit roof-room isn't world enough for him.

When he's ready, he emerges. Like a queen he descends the red carpet of the main staircase, forbidden to kitchen staff. He has done his best, shaving carefully and using the magnifying side of the mirror to apply his foundation. His eyeshadow is blue, his lipstick and high heels scarlet. It isn't an outrageous skirt, just an ordinary one, giving that extraordinarily vulnerable sensation that all women must feel. If you pass close to him, his confidence smells of gin, a thin hard note within the cheap perfume.

People start pointing and muttering even before he enters the darkened function room which has been re-arranged as a supper-dance suite. The girl on the door isn't sure if he's allowed in, but in the absence of instructions to the contrary she lets him in.

Not that he's doing anything wrong, sitting with a gin and tonic, his white plastic handbag on his arm, his legs crossed, one scarlet toe swinging almost nonchalantly to the rhythm of the drums and accordion. He doesn't dare meet anyone's eye. He knows they're looking and part of him is pleased, part afraid. But he's doing no harm. He doesn't expect to be asked to dance. He just wants to sit and watch and feel like a woman.

The disturbance is swirling towards him; he's used to its approach. In the midst of it, within the sweet melody of the Evie Two-step, the boss's fury can be felt. He fights his way to Henry's table and grabs him by the arm, spilling his drink.

'You scum!' he spits. 'Get out! Now! I won't have dirt

here! You're fired – you've got till midday tomorrow to get out of my hotel, or I'll have the police on you!'

'Excuse me,' Henry says calmly. 'I've dropped my bag.'

He must not lose his dignity.

'Damn your bloody bag!'

The boss aims his foot at it and it goes skiting off under the table legs, knocked this way and that until it's lost.

Much to the affronted delight of the guests, Henry is unceremoniously evicted, wig askew, staggering, trying to retain his composure.

'But I've paid to get in!'

'I don't care what you've paid for. You're not going to give my hotel a filthy reputation for harbouring perverts like you! Go on! Get out! And don't let me see you again!'

Henry struts bravely off towards the kitchen and back stairs. But later, if you glanced along the shadowy attic landing, you'd see Henry outside his door, slumped like an abandoned Hallowe'en guy, waiting for the sounds of the dance to die away. Then he creeps down the dark back stairs, through the kitchens and into the gloomy function room beyond, where he crawls about on his hands and knees until he finds his handbag which mercifully has stayed shut. It has been stood on and is sticky with drinks and dirt. His compact is shattered, but now he can get into his room.

So once more Henry's packing what little he has, ready to move on again. He has arrived and left so many times that he no longer has feelings for rooms. They all feel impassive, as if they know they'll not be allowed to keep him.

The news travels quickly and by morning everyone knows he's going. Lizzie is gleeful, Mac is dourly satisfied, Mrs Dorrie breathes alcohol and sympathy over him. The summer waitresses regret the passing of a diversion.

Carol, an elfin summer waitress, has been kinder than most to him. She at least listened to him, and he never actually caught her laughing at him. To her, he gives the key of his room. He knows she is sleeping in a wooden panelled area beside the lift mechanism until the boss gets a caravan for the extra staff. At least she'll be more comfortable in a bed.

Fortunately he is paid what is owed to him, but not a penny more. Usually you get a bonus for good work. He knows his work isn't what's taken into account.

Carol is touched that Henry's giving her his room.

'Henry, isn't there some way you could be helped? Can't you have an operation or something?'

'I'd have had it years ago if I could have, love. Doctors have got no time for the likes of me. Quite right too, maybe. Heal the sick.'

'Where'll you go?'

'Oh, maybe Skye.'

'Don't you think you'd get on better nearer home?'

'Home!' he laughed. 'If I'd a home I'd be staying there!'

'No, but London, I mean, it's a big place. You might not get so much hostility.'

'Be nice to think so, love, wouldn't it! Must be going now. Ta ta for now!'

And off he goes, everything he owns in one of those little round-cornered ladies overnight cases; sad and ordinary in a navy three-quarter-length jacket.

A weight seems to have been lifted. Teenie is giving everyone cigarettes, Robbie compliments her lingeringly, Flora nabs three chance tables and allows Carol the fourth. Mac whistles as he butchers the sheep's carcase which has been dripping pinkly onto the butter pots in the cold store for the last couple of days. Chips of bone fly from the marble table-top to all corners of the kitchen. Lizzie scrubs pots and potatoes in a black fury with everyone.

In the evening they're all run off their feet with dinners. Even Mrs Dorrie is helping Mac out. In the midst of the chaos a raucous voice is heard and Henry, in full regalia, stumbles gratefully into the kitchen.

'Get that bastard out of here!' Mac yells, salvaging a dropped steak from the floor.

Henry puts his arms round Carol, who is looking at him in anguish. He kisses her ear and her eye. 'A good girl, love . . .'

'Henry, lad, we're a peedie bit busy. You'll have to go now, before the boss hears you,' Mrs Dorrie pleads.

'Nowhere to go!' Henry yells thickly. 'No money.'

He stumbles over to Mrs Dorrie and fumbles at her.

'Suckle me . . . suckle me . . .' he sobs, sliding to the floor. 'Just want you to love me . . . just sleep here . . .'

He pillows her feet and lies quietly.

'Henry, laddie, you'll need to be moving.'

The boss knows Henry's been drinking in his downstairs bar all day. He doesn't mind his money coming back to him. He calls the police as soon as he hears Henry yelling.

The policeman hauls him to his feet. The boss looks on, beetroot furious, speechless. Henry's dragged out to the corridor and begins to struggle. A scuffle. Henry starts crying, noisily. Sobbing, crying to be loved. Then furious. Hard knocks and bangs and noises of pain. Then Henry is hauled off in handcuffs, broken, again.

In his room, Carol finds a polystyrene wig stand and the red high heel shoes. The faceless white head frightens her so she gives it to Teenie, but she leaves the shoes untouched in the bottom drawer. They would only be ridiculed and somehow they deserve a little respite.

When she leaves, people will think they were hers. Henry would have liked that.

BIOGRAPHICAL NOTES

WILLIAM ANDREW was born in Glasgow in 1931. He taught English in London and Glasgow, and in the 1970s had several radio plays and two stage plays produced. In 1979, with the help of a Scottish Arts Council bursary, he began writing full-time. Since then he has worked mainly for television – three half-hour plays in STV's *Preview* series, various school programmes, and many episodes of the serial *Take the High Road*.

GEORGE MACKAY BROWN has always lived in Orkney. He has published seven collections of poems (most recently *Christmas Poems*, 1984), three novels (including *Time in a Red Coat*, 1984), three books of legends and stories for young people, two collections of short stories (*Andrina*, 1983 and *Christmas Stories*, 1985) and several plays. He has numerous other literary projects in various stages of completion.

MOIRA BURGESS was born in Campbeltown in 1936 and is a full-time writer and mother. Her novel *The Day Before Tomorrow* was published in 1971. She compiled *The Glasgow Novel: a bibliography* (1972: second edition forthcoming) and co-edited *Streets of Stone* (Salamander Press 1985), an anthology of Glasgow short stories. For some years she wrote mainly articles, but a Scottish Arts Council bursary in 1982 encouraged her to return to fiction, and short stories have been published in *Scottish Short Stories 1985*, *New Writing Scotland 2 & 3*, and the collection of Scottish women's writing, *Original Prints* (Polygon 1985).

KIRKPATRICK DOBIE was born in Dumfries in 1908. His work has appeared in earlier volumes of *Scottish Short Stories*, but he is known chiefly for his collections of poetry: *A Fatal Tree*, 1971; *Like Tracks of Birds*, 1976; *That Other Life*, 1980; *Poems From a Provincial Town*, 1983; *Against the Tide*, 1985. He is a retired grain merchant.

MAUREEN DUFF was born and educated in Glasgow, and holds an MA in English and Philosophy. In 1983 she was the runner-up in the *Cosmopolitan* New Journalists' Competition, and in 1984 she won the *Woman's Own* Fiction Competition with 'Krakatoa, East of Java'. Her articles and illustrations have been published in several magazines, and she has contributed an article on travelling in Hawaii to *Half the Earth*, a travel book for women (1986). She works in a theatrical agency in north London.

AUDREY EVANS was born and brought up in St Andrews and graduated from St Andrews University before becoming a drama teacher. She now lives in the East Neuk of Fife, has had six plays published, several stories broadcast (among them, 'Mossy'), and has just completed an historical novel.

PATRICK FARNON was born in Hamilton, Scotland and lives with his wife and daughter in Amsterdam where he has been working for more than ten years as a journalist. Previous stories have appeared in *Stand*, *Scottish Book of Short Stories*, *New Edinburgh Review*, *Words*, *Scotsman Magazine* and other small magazines.

RONALD FRAME was born in 1953 in Glasgow and educated there and at Oxford. He is the author of two books, the novel *Winter Journey* (1984), and the collection of short stories *Watching Mrs Gordon* (1985, both The Bodley Head). A second collection of short prose is due to be published later this year, followed by a new novel in 1987. His work has been dramatized on television and radio.

ALEX. HAMILTON was born in Glasgow in 1949. He writes and reads stories, and composes and sings songs. His main preoccupation is finding a publisher for his novel.

IAIN CAMERON MACDONALD was born in Edinburgh in 1960, and was educated at Greenock Academy and Glasgow University, where he took an MA in English. He now lives with his wife and daughter in Herefordshire where he teaches English.

LORN MACINTYRE was born in Argyll. A full-time writer, he now lives near St Andrews.

CATRIONA MALAN, born in 1942, has spent most of her life in Helensburgh, where she lives with her eighteen-year-old son and works as a primary school teacher. In 1984 she joined her local Writers' Workshop and began writing poetry. More recently she has become interested in the writing of short stories.

IAN RANKIN was born in Cardenden. Fife, in 1960. He is a postgraduate student at Edinburgh University, and his short stories have appeared in the *Scotsman*, the *Edinburgh Review*, *Cencrastus*, the *Scottish Review*, *New Writing Scotland 2 & 3*, and have been broadcast on Radio 4. In

1984 he won the Radio Forth/TSB Scotland Short Story Competition, and this enabled him to enjoy a holiday in Egypt, where 'Scarab' was born. His first novel, *The Flood*, was published by Polygon Books earlier this year, and his second, *Knots and Crosses*, will be published by The Bodley Head in 1987.

DILYS ROSE was born in Glasgow in 1954. Since 1974 she has travelled and worked in a variety of countries and occupations. At present, Edinburgh is her home. She was awarded a Writer's Bursary by the Scottish Arts Council in September 1985.

IAIN CRICHTON SMITH was born in 1928 on the island of Lewis in the Outer Hebrides. He writes, both in Gaelic and English, plays, novels, poems and short stories. His most recent novel in English, *The Tenement*, was published by Gollancz in 1985, and his *Selected Poems* by Carcanet the same year.

ALEXANDER MCCALL SMITH was born in 1948 in Zimbabwe and educated both there and in Scotland. Previous short stories have appeared in a number of journals and collections, including *Scottish Short Stories 1984*. His collection of African traditional stories, *Children of Wax*, was originally broadcast by the BBC and is now being filmed. He is the author of ten published books, and is currently Associate Dean of the Faculty of Law at Edinburgh University. He is married, with one daughter.

IAN SPRING was born in Glasgow and studied at Strathclyde, Glasgow and Edinburgh Universities. He is the author of several articles on literature and folklore and lives in Rutherglen with his wife and daughter.

VALERIE THORNTON was born in Glasgow in 1954, and educated in Stirling and Glasgow, where she studied English and Drama. Since then she has worked on two feature films shot in Glasgow, for the Scottish Film Council and the Edinburgh Film Festival, and has taught English for five years. Her stories have been published in *New Writing Scotland 1, 2 & 3*, *Streets of Stone*, *Scottish Review*, and the *Glasgow Magazine*. Her poems have appeared in *Lines Review*, *PN Review*, *International PEN*, *Cyphers* (Eire) and the *Wascana Review* (Canada).